James Philip

Main Force Country

UNTIL THE NIGHT – BOOK ONE

Copyright © James P. Coldham writing as James Philip, in respect of Main Force Country, Book 1 of the Until the Night Series (the serialisation of the 2nd Edition of Until the Night), 2015. All rights reserved.

Cover concept by James Philip
Graphic Design by Beastleigh Web Design

———

The Bomber War Series

Book 1: Until the Night
Book 2: The Painter
Book 3: The Cloud Walkers

Until the Night Series

A serialisation of Book 1: Until the Night in five parts

Part 1: Main Force Country – September 1943
Part 2: The Road to Berlin – October 1943
Part 3: The Big City – November 1943
Part 4: When Winter Comes – December 1943
Part 5: After Midnight – January 1944

Main Force Country

The Nazis entered this war under the rather childish delusion that they were going to bomb everyone else, and nobody was going to bomb them. At Rotterdam, London, Warsaw and half a hundred other places, they put their rather naive theory into operation. They sowed the wind, and now they are going to reap the whirlwind.

A lot of people (generally those with no qualifications to speak, if to think) are in the habit of iterating the silly phrase 'bombing can never win the war'. Well, we shall see. It hasn't been tried yet...

Air Marshall Sir Arthur Harris
[Air Officer Commanding-in-Chief RAF Bomber Command]

Prologue

Monday 18th December, 1939 - RAF Faldwell, Norfolk

"THERE!" Somebody called. "COMING IN OVER THE VILLAGE!"

Every man on the watchtower balcony looked southward; every eye peered hard into the deepening grey dusk. No breath of wind stirred the icy fens and a clammy mist rose like smoke off the water as the first stars twinkled in the cold clear eastern sky.

The Wellingtons had arrived in Norfolk in May; big black impressively powerful twin-engine modern aircraft to replace the Squadron's long obsolete, lumbering Handley Page Harrows. In September, on the first afternoon of the war the gleaming new bombers had sortied in a rush of excitement and wholly misplaced bravura. Their first mission was a fool's errand, a speculative, unsuccessful hunt for elements of the German fleet off Helgoland, and somehow, despite flying perilously close to a string of Luftwaffe fighter fields, Faldwell's Wellingtons had returned unblooded to East Anglia.

That was over three months ago.

Since then 380 Squadron had settled into an uneasy, and in many ways faintly absurd, 'hostilities' routine. In fact relatively little distinguished the new regimen from the old, pre-war ways; although air raid drills became a regular, somewhat irksome feature of station life, and every now and again a lucky crew was actually allowed to drop a single small 'live' bomb on the nearby range at Upton St Thomas. Otherwise, life at Faldwell carried on as it always had. Yet if life in the Norfolk fens went on more or less as it always had, elsewhere the war rumbled distantly and already there were ill omens aplenty to nurture the dark forebodings of those who recognised the deceptively 'phoney' nature of the war for what it inevitably presaged. While the Squadron had kicked its heels Poland had fallen, U-47 had slipped into Scapa Flow and sunk the battleship Royal Oak, and in France the British Expeditionary Force – a handful of sketchily equipped Divisions superbly equipped to fight the last war and representing pretty much the entire available fighting strength of the British Army – was digging in beside the French, attempting to fill much of the yawning gap between the northern end of the vaunted Maginot Line and the Channel coast. Thus far Faldwell's war had been completely bloodless, completely phoney, and until today complacency had ruled supreme.

The approaching bomber was very low,

flying on one engine. A red flare arched lazily across the stars and drifted slowly down to earth. *Wounded onboard.* There had been no word from any of the Squadron's Wellingtons for over five hours. Nor despite repeated inquiries, from Group Headquarters at Exning, near Newmarket.

"Dammit! Where are the others?" The Station Commander, Group Captain Crowe-Martin, a short, dapper veteran of the Royal Flying Corps demanded. He was a relative newcomer, his face still deeply tanned from a two year posting in Palestine. Like many experienced officers he had been called home at the outbreak of war. "Dammit! Why aren't the aerodrome lights on?"

Nobody, it seemed, had thought of turning on the lights. Why would they? The Squadron never flew at night. Night flying was forbidden. It was far too hazardous, and in any event, Faldwell's Wellingtons were day bombers and the crews were not trained to fly at night.

Binoculars scanned the horizon.

"Can anybody make out who it is?"

"It might be T, sir."

T-Tommy was Flight-Lieutenant Pat Farlane's kite. "Good old Pat," muttered an anonymous voice in the background as the crippled bomber came in so low it seemed to skim the rooftops of the cottages beyond the perimeter fence. It wobbled over two parked Tiger Moth trainers, its port wing tip dipping perilously close to the ground.

"He's got his wheels up!" Yelped the controller. "Somebody call out the fire engine!"

Group Captain Crowe-Martin gripped the balcony railing. He was fighting a losing battle to contain his rage. His whole body was trembling. Had nobody thought of calling out the fire engine or the ambulance before now? This was the blind were leading the blind!

He had been at Faldwell little more than a fortnight and notwithstanding his whipcord flashing temper and terrier like energy, it had been impossible in such a short time to make more than a start putting right the shamefully deep-seated inadequacies of his predecessor's abruptly curtailed tenure. Crowe-Martin had seen enough action in France in 1918, and in 'policing' operations on the Northwest Frontier and the Middle-East since to recognise exactly how ill-prepared his new command was for war. The Germans had learned their business in Spain; and all the evidence suggested that they had ruthlessly put their experience to good use in Poland. The men he had sent out that afternoon were no less brave than their foes, and almost certainly as technically proficient in many respects, but they were innocents riding for a terrible fall. Now as he watched the station swing – in chaotic, dislocated slow motion – into action he was unhappily reminded of scenes from the Keystone Cops movies he had so loved as a younger man.

It was not his fault but it was no less humiliating for it.

'It is a mess,' the Group Commander had told him bluntly the day he took command at Faldwell. The AOC was a no-nonsense man with few illusions about what lay ahead. Moreover, he made no secret of the fact. 'We weren't ready for war three months ago, and frankly, we're no nearer to being ready now! We're short of everything. Aircraft, bombs, men. And even if we had the tools to do the job the blasted politicians can't make up their minds what we should be bombing!'

Group Captain Crowe-Martin had never been a member of the 'it'll all be over by Christmas' brigade. Nevertheless, he was a little shocked by his superior's candour.

'Surely things aren't all black, sir?'

'No, of course not.' The AOC had sighed, paused to dig out a cigarette, a Camel. 'The crews are fine fellows. The best. We must not let them down.' There had been a tinge of regret, almost resignation in the Group Commander's gruff words. 'The thing is we must use what time we have to train the crews. Prepare them for the day the gloves come off.' He had removed his reading glasses, placed them on his desk and sat back in his chair. 'When you get to Faldwell I want you to light a bonfire under the station! I don't want flying clubs in my Group, I want fighting squadrons! Fighting squadrons!'

For Faldwell the 'phoney war' finally came to an abrupt end the moment T-Tommy hit the ground half-a-mile distant from the watchtower. The Wellington skidded into the middle distance in a cloud of smoke, shedding splintered metal and spreading mud in its wake. The stricken bomber slewed around, slid sideways across the grass, gouging a shallow furrow, and slithered to a halt in the approximate centre of the airfield, steaming. Mercifully, there was no fire, nor an explosion because the brightly polished, immaculately burnished and endlessly inspected – for traces of grime, oil, and specks of dust, the engine was rarely fired up because it tended to get dirty - fire engine had stalled, shuddering to a hissing, clanking standstill in front of the nearest of Faldwell's three big C Type hangars. The ambulance trundled past it, sedately, bumping over the turf, wheels churning up the ground.

"I can see chaps baling out of T," reported the controller, binoculars glued to his eyes.

"One, two, three, four. No, five! They're carrying some poor fellow..."

The fire wagon was moving again at last, wheezing, backfiring, its bell ringing apologetically. Belatedly, the flare path lights blinked into life. The inky sky was eerily silent, empty. Group Captain Crowe-Martin, sighed, scowled and without a word headed for the flight room. He suspected, they all suspected that something awful had happened and he wanted to be the first to hear the worst of it. The Adjutant, a large, clumsy man followed him down the watchtower steps, hurrying to keep up as his Station Commander marched briskly towards the long, low, red-brick building next to the hangars.

Presently, Flight-Lieutenant Pat Farlane led three other bruised, battered, variously shaken members of his crew into the flight room. Outwardly, the pilot was calm, a lighted cigarette in one hand, the other distractedly preening the lovingly cultivated bushy handlebars of his moustache. He straightened when he saw the Station Master.

"Stand easy," Crowe-Martin rasped. "What the bloody hell happened?"

"The flight out was okay, sir," Farlane shrugged; beneath the sang-froid he was ashen-faced and dull-eyed. "We stooged around over the German Bight a while. At least an hour. Eventually, we bombed some destroyers from about fifteen thousand feet. No idea if we hit anything. I doubt it, personally. Hard enough hitting a factory from that height let alone a target twisting and turning at thirty knots." A brief pause, a drag on his cigarette. "Pretty soon after that the fighters turned up. Single-engine jobs first, Messerschmitt 109s, then big twin-engine beggars, 110s. The CO's kite bought it early on. Lost an engine and fell out of formation and got set on by half-a-dozen 109s. Like a pack of wolves upon the fold." This remark he punctuated with a weary grimace. "Poor fellow didn't have a chance. My gunners ran out of ammo after about half-an-hour. The Jerries didn't, of course. I think Bill Tomlinson's kite was the last to buy it."

The Station Commander listened impassively. Squadron Leader Bill Tomlinson, a bluff, big-hearted man in his mid-thirties, commanded A Flight. Crowe-Martin had often rubbed shoulders with his elder brother, Freddie, in the bar of the King David Hotel in Jerusalem. Freddie Tomlinson was a true salt of the earth and he had subsequently discovered Bill to be a man broken out of exactly the same mould, fine company.

"They just kept coming," Farlane went on, hands shaking, now. "They followed us all the way back. They only gave up when the coast was in sight. G was the last to go down. Poor old George, bloody good kite was George. Took a hell of a pasting from a couple of 110s and blew up. It just blew up. One minute it was there. The next, bang! We were above and a tad behind George's wing. Something hit my starboard engine. Next thing I knew the bloody thing had seized up on me. Poor old Bert Fulshawe was in formation right behind George. Copped the lot. I thought Bert was a goner, I can tell you. I couldn't believe my eyes when Bert came out the other side."

"What happened to Squadron Leader Fulshawe's aircraft?" Crowe-Martin barked. Bert Fulshawe was B Flight Commander, and deputy CO of 380 Squadron. He was married to the daughter of a local worthy, a strikingly attractive, rather aloof girl who was invariably the main focus of attention when the Mess entertained.

"Bert got the old girl down on the beach at Southwold, sir."

"You saw R-Robert land?"

"Ditched in the surf, close to the shore. Seemed to be in one piece. More or less..."

"What about our other aircraft?"

Farlane paused, swallowed hard.

"All gone, sir."

"Get through to Southwold," Crowe-Martin

barked, turning to the Adjutant. "Find out what's happened to R-Robert's crew. Try the Police and the Army first. If we have to we'll send out our own search party." An afterthought: "Who was flying as Bert's second pilot?"

"Er, I don't know, sir," the Adjutant admitted. "I can find out, sir."

Farlane coughed. "Chantrey," he said. "Pilot Officer Adam Chantrey, sir."

"Of course," the Station Commander sighed, "cocky little so and so..."

Chapter 1

Wednesday 22nd September, 1943
RAF Waltham Grange, Lincolnshire

"FIGHTER STARBOARD! CORKSCREW PORT. NOW! NOW! NOW!"

It had been a quiet trip until then but there was terror, raw and feral in the rear gunner's voice. Panic in its purest, unrefined state because the fighter was close. Point blank range. Down below the tail. In a moment it would pull up, hang on its props and pour cannon fire into R-Robert's exposed belly.

They were doomed.

He reacted with the desperation of a cornered, hunted animal. Hurling the Lancaster into a vertical bank to port he stamped on the left rudder bar; thrust the starboard throttles through the gate. The bomber fell into space, shuddering with the recoil of the gunners' Brownings. The engines screamed, the bomber's over-stressed airframe groaned.

The first time he had corkscrewed a Lancaster - without holding back, that was - the starboard wing-tip had sheared off. That was in another lifetime, in broad daylight three miles high over Salisbury Plain not in the stygian darkness of the German night. The squadrons had reported a number of unexplained crashes and he had been ordered to 'look into it.' Oh, and assuming he lived long enough 'to report back.' The corkscrew had done the trick, solved the mystery once and for all. There had been an ominous CRACK. The controls had momentarily gone slack, kicked back at him. Landing twenty minutes later at Boscombe Down the starboard aileron, its outer end secured by a single bent retaining pin, had fallen off halfway down the runway. Had it fallen off when the wing tip had parted company with the aircraft high above Littleton Down, or at any time before the wheels touched ground, he would have bought it. There and then...

Now something behind him creaked loudly.
CRACK.
He shut it out.
CRACK...

If the wings came off, the wings came off. There was absolutely nothing he could do about it so there was no point worrying about it. It was the luck of the game. Maybe it was their turn to die tonight, maybe not.

"HE'S FOLLOWING US DOWN! GO STARBOARD! NOW! NOW!"

He hauled the controls to the right with every ounce of his strength. The nose lifted, the aircraft juddered, he jammed the port throttles hard up against the stops. R-Robert reared into a gut-wrenching, climbing turn to starboard.

Somewhere in the near distance the fighter twisted and turned, engines throttled back to stalling point battling to hold the silhouette of the tumbling Lancaster in the cross-hairs of its gun sight. Normally the first corkscrew - assuming it was executed with suicidal gusto - sufficed. The fighter overshot and disappeared into the darkness. Life went on. Unfortunately, this fellow knew his business. This fellow was no fumbling novice out for a quick kill. This fellow was a gimlet-eyed cove. This fellow enjoyed his work. This fellow had a bone in his teeth, ice in his soul and murder in mind.

The gunner's next warning cleaved the night.

"FIGHTER ATTACKING! GO PORT!"

He had already applied maximum opposite rudder. The fighter would try to turn inside the heavy. It was now or never. Claim the kill or stall out. Bomber and fighter might as easily collide, neither aircraft was actually under control – not at least in any fashion envisaged by their respective designers - and it only took a fractional misjudgement. Behind him bodies were thrown across the fuselage, first one way then the other, thudding, groaning. The flight engineer or the navigator. Perhaps, both of them.

No time to turn, or to pause, look around.

Nor even to panic.

No time for anything.

Tracer, blue and white, flashed overhead. The Perspex panel above his left shoulder shattered. R-Robert staggered, reeled drunkenly as 20-millimetre cannon shells raked her. Each impact jarred the control column. In a moment the cockpit filled with the acrid stench of burnt cordite.

"HE'S COMING ROUND AGAIN!" Yelled the rear gunner, looking death in the eye, unhinged. "CORKSCREW STARBOARD! NOW! NOW!"

There were flames in the cockpit and somewhere behind him, raging. He could feel the heat at his back. It was all over, it was hopeless. Still he fought on. That was what you did, even when it was too late. You never gave in. Never.

He stood the heavy on its starboard wingtip, yanked back on the right-hand throttles, kicked savagely at the rudder bar. The Lancaster screamed into the dive. Steeper and steeper, faster and faster. The controls were frozen, immovable in his hands. No matter how hard he hauled back on the column the Lancaster fell, plummeting into the abyss. He watched in disbelieving horror as the airspeed indicator foretold his death. R-Robert rattled, the slipstream thundered, her Merlins raced. He had to get out, bale out, but he could not move. The death dive pinned him in his seat. What about the others?

"BALE OUT! BALE OUT!"

It was too late. The fire was all around him, burning, licking, consuming. The tendrils of flames twisted and writhed, wrapped him in their embrace. Oddly, there was no pain, nothing but despair. A cold, terrible despair...and anger.

"BALE OUT!"

Every muscle cried out in protest. He was trapped. No matter how he tore at the controls, struggled to free himself he could not move. He was frozen, pinned in his seat, the cockpit his fiery coffin. Far, far away another city burned and by the flickering, sickly orange light of its fires he saw the dark ground rushing up to meet him. The cries of the maimed and the dying filled the intercom.

The flames reached for him.

"NO!" It was the way it was always going to end and he had known it from the start. "NO!" No sound came from his lips. "NO..."

Wing-Commander Adam Chantrey awakened in a cold sweat.

It was pitch black in his quarters. He took

a series of long, slow breaths to calm his racing thoughts. Beads of perspiration trickled down his brow. His cot was a shambles, the sheets strewn about him and on the floor.

"Oh, God..."

Presently, his pulse slowed, the blind terror subsided. He groped unsteadily for his cigarette case on the small, rickety table at the head of the bed and swung his long legs over the side of the cot. His hands shook when he lit up. They shook so badly it took him several attempts to light the cigarette.

He stared into the darkness. Each time the nightmare was different. Everybody knew bad dreams were an occupational hazard. Part and parcel of flying ops, but lately, his dreams came more often and their effects lingered longer. Insidiously, corrosively. The funny thing was that when he was flying ops regularly he dreamed less, and sometimes went several nights without a nightmare. It was as if flying ops exorcised some inner demon. He smoked his cigarette.

It was three weeks since the Squadron had last flown an op. Mannheim. In the interregnum the Moon and the weather had conspired to ground the Main Force and the enforced inactivity had made them all a little bit twitchy.

It was a little after six o'clock.

Knowing it was pointless trying to get back to sleep Adam got to his feet. He washed and shaved in icy water, donned his battledress. Rufus, his black wolf of a German Shepherd remained curled in his basket, viewing his master with sleepily attentive eyes.

"Walkies!" Adam muttered, pulling on his greatcoat and retrieving his gloves from its pockets. The Alsatian roused himself, stretched.

The blackness of the eastern sky was fading to twilight as man and dog strolled towards the dispersals beyond the hangars. The clouds were high and the wind had dropped to a whisper overnight. A thin, low mist lay on the ground. *Ops weather*. There would almost certainly be a major attack tonight. Hundreds of miles to the east the dawn would have already broken over the German cities.

Two erks on bicycles rode by in the gloom, saluting awkwardly without stopping. The station was waking up.

"Breakfast time," decided the commander of No. 388 (Heavy) Bomber Squadron, thinking out aloud.

Chapter 2

Wednesday 22nd September, 1943
The Gatekeeper's Lodge, Ansham Wolds, Lincolnshire

Eleanor dropped two pieces of newly chopped wood onto the fire. It had been wet recently and the logs were damp. The wood sizzled and crackled, spat in the hearth.

Lancasters were taking off from the surrounding airfields. Each bomber's passage rattled the windows and set the cottage softly trembling. Eleanor waited for the children to wake, to call out for her. In the beginning the sound and fury of the Lancasters setting off for Germany had terrified them but lately they slept blissfully through the racket.

She settled in the threadbare armchair by the fire and sipped her weak cocoa. She was tired; it had been a long day. First Emily, her youngest, had picked over her breakfast and complained of a sore throat. Then the key had broken in the padlock to the Church Hall door, preventing her opening the school on time. While she was still sorting that out Jonathan, her eldest, had fallen out with one of the evacuees, an older boy called Dennis Chester.

'It wasn't my fault, Missis Grafton!' The little urchin had pleaded, quaking with fear once she had separated the six and seven year old pugilists. Eleanor's predecessor at the village school had ruled her little empire not so much with a rod as with a leather strap, which she had hung, threateningly, and very prominently, on a hook next to the blackboard. Eleanor had thrown away the strap the day she took over the school. That morning she had contented herself with delivering a stern telling off - her father liked to remind her she had 'a talent for putting strong men in their places', let alone miscreant children – and ordered the boys to shake hands. She had taken the additional precaution of sitting them as far apart as possible for the rest of the day.

'For goodness sake, boys!' She had exclaimed, exasperated. 'Do you not think there are enough people in the world at each other's throats already without you two joining in?'

The boys had stared at their feet, nodded sulkily. Poor Dennis Chester had not stopped shaking until long after he realised that there was to be no beating. Her Johnny, much the smaller of the two boys, had glanced this way and that, horribly embarrassed.

Eleanor was worried about Johnny.

Her son had been too young to understand what was going on when his father had been killed. Her husband, Harry, had gone overseas when his son was only three and Johnny had few if any memories of him. Then when her brother, David, had been shot down over Wismar last year he had gone into his shell, become withdrawn, awkward. Although Johnny had slowly come out of it, there were still too many days like today when she could do nothing with him.

Eleanor stifled a yawn, picked up her father's letter. She had read it quickly that morning; not had another opportunity since. The letter was dated 18th September.

Dear Eleanor,

I'm sorry I've not written for a while. I've been a little under the weather and completely rushed off my feet at the Ministry. There is always so much to do and never enough time!

Would it be convenient for me to pay you a visit in a week or so? I'd hope to come up to Lincolnshire on Monday 27th. If anything comes up in the meantime I'll send you a telegram - just so you don't go to the trouble of making preparations for nothing.

My doctor says I should take a few days off. Get plenty of fresh air and so on. I described Ansham Wolds to him and he said it sounds just the ticket.

Forgive me if this puts you out. Please let me know if it does, I won't be offended. I know how involved in things you are in the village and that you cannot just abandon everything at the drop of a hat.

If I do come up I shall probably catch an early train. There's a connection at Lincoln that will get me into Thurlby-le-Wold around about 11:00. If you could meet me I'd be obliged, some days are better than others but now and then I'm still a little bit wobbly on my pins.

One piece of news since I saw you last.

I have finally received another letter from David. Much censored, I'm afraid. He is well. It seems he's been transferred to a Stalag Luft (that's a camp run by the Luftwaffe for captured enemy airmen). Apparently he's met a lot of old chums! All the names are inked out of course, but I've worked out who one or two of the other chaps are. He is in good company. He sounds cheerful and is obviously trying to make the best of a bad deal. Being wholly selfish, I'm glad he's safe although I'm sure David doesn't see it quite like that and I wouldn't dream of saying as much outside the family. I'd hoped to bring the letter with me when I came up to see you. Unfortunately, it contains one or two cryptic references - which may or may not be some sort of coded message - so I've passed the letter to the intelligence people. Just in case it is anything important.

Please give my love to the children.
All my love,
Father.

"Oh, Father," she murmured, out aloud. "You never change." Of course he was 'putting her out'. She had a hundred things on her plate, nor was she in any position to drop what she was doing. Nevertheless, she was already looking forward to seeing him again. The children would be excited. It would be lovely to have him staying at the cottage. Lovely to be a family together. Lovely to remind themselves of what they still had and to forget for a few days at least, what they had all lost.

More Lancasters were taking off in the night.

When she finished her cocoa she would go outside and check the blackout screen on the parlour window. Her tormentor, Mr Rowbotham, the village's Chief ARP - Air Raid Precautions - Warden, claimed he had detected a chink of light escaping on two nights recently. Of course, the horrible little man had not had the courage to knock on her door and confront her with the allegation. The first she had known about it was a letter threatening her with a thirty shilling fine if she 'failed to take immediate and effective remedial action'.

Over Lincolnshire scores - possibly hundreds - of bombers were now climbing into the heavens.

The Rector had confided to her that many years ago Harry's father had had a run in with the Rowbothams. The feud went back at least twenty years. It was so long ago he could not recollect the nature of the problem or dispute, simply that after some years the Rowbothams had been evicted from the tenancy of Edge Farm, which had in any event, now completely disappeared beneath the footprint of the new aerodrome.

'Edward Rowbotham,' the Rector explained, 'isn't a mean-spirited fellow. Not like his father, Herbert. Herbert drank, and it brought the worst out of him. Edward's teetotal. A little humourless, perhaps because he's teetotal. But he's not a bad man. Overly fastidious, a little petty, admittedly. I'm sure he's not out to settle old scores. That wouldn't be like him at all.'

Whenever Eleanor checked the cottage's

blackout it was perfect. The Gatekeeper's Lodge was only a mile or so from the airfield so she had always taken care – the most painstaking meticulous care - over the blackout. Screens for the big windows, blackened sticky paper for the smaller ones, heavy, double drapes everywhere.

"Blast the silly little man!" She seethed, inwardly. As if she did not have enough to worry about. The Rector had warned her against having it out with Mr Rowbotham. 'These things easily get out of hand,' he had pointed out.

He was right, of course. She would double check the blackout, do whatever was necessary to satisfy Mr Rowbotham. The next time she met him in the village she would smile nicely, thank him for his vigilance and politely promise to make amends.

Eleanor had moved up to Lincolnshire three years ago when Harry had gone overseas and Emmy was still a baby in arms. At that time Bomber Command's presence was mainly in the south of the county, now the whole of Lincolnshire was Bomber Command Country. Sprawling to the north and south of Lincoln were the respective fiefdoms of 1 and 5 Groups. The names of many of the airfields were quaint, possessed of a particular Englishness that everybody tended to take for granted: Ansham Wolds, Bardney, Binbrook, Blyton, Conningsby, Dunholme Lodge, Elsham Wolds, Faldingworth, Fiskerton, Hemswell, Holton-le-Clay, Ludford Magna, Kelmington, Kirmington, Metherington, Scampton, Skellingthorpe, Spilsby, Swinderby, Upton, Waddington, Waltham Grange and Woodall Spa. Some of the names were already passing into legend and others would follow before the war was over. Astride the Lincolnshire Wold, Ansham Wolds, and its neighbours, Elsham Wolds and Kirmington, were the most northerly enclaves of 1 Group.

Lincolnshire, the county of flowers, was an unlikely front-line. At night the clamour of Lancasters climbing in the night fell down to earth like a sign from the gods, an awesome and terrible thing; the harbinger of ruin. In the small hours of the morning countless returning heavies clattered low across the rooftops, rattling souls and windows, turning majestically in the cold grey dawn about the towers of Lincoln's great hill-top cathedral and racing for home. No matter how hard Eleanor tried to pretend otherwise the bombers were now a part of her life.

Her father was a senior principal scientific officer at the Air Ministry. Although he never spoke about his work her brother had let slip, in tipsy moments, that he was 'fairly high up' in something called 'radio counter-measures', and spent a lot of time 'hobnobbing' with the 'brass at Command.' Whatever that meant! Dave always seemed to speak in code as if native English was his second language, and most of the time Eleanor had had no real idea what he was talking about.

Dave had been shot down on his twenty-third op.

Eleanor gazed into the hearth. The damp logs had stopped spitting but even as the warmth of the fire touched her pale cheeks, she shivered involuntarily.

It was the coming of the bombers that had belatedly dragged the sleepy little hamlet of Ansham Wolds - and to a lesser extent, nearby Kingston Magna - into the mainstream of the twentieth century and face to face with the tragedy of the age. In all its history the world had, more or less, passed Ansham Wolds by and moved on without ever troubling to look back until that fateful day in January 1941 that the Air Ministry surveyors had come to the village. Their visit had signalled the end of the old ways for ever. At that time the men from the Ministry had come and gone almost unnoticed but not before they had identified a large tract of land north-east of the village eminently well-appointed for their purpose.

Much of the land on which the aerodrome –

RAF Ansham Wolds - now stood had once, before Eleanor's time, been Grafton land. Whatever her father had thought of Harry Grafton, nobody could accuse her of marrying him for his money. Harry never had any money and what little he had tended to escape through his fingers like quicksilver.

The country around Ansham Wolds was sparsely-wooded, dominated by open, bleak fields and barren, virgin wolds. The site the surveyors had identified was some four miles from Thurlby Junction, where the east-west LNER – London and North Eastern Railway - line from South Yorkshire to the coast met the line coming up from Lincoln and Gainsborough in the south. As if the existence of a nearby rail head was not enough the site was situated less than two miles north of a major trunk road, the A18, which linked Scunthorpe in the west with Grimsby in the east. A well-drained, flat expanse of land close to an established rail head and a major road, and several miles from the nearest large town was exactly what the RAF was looking for and the land was acquired with indecent, rather un-British haste. The men from the Ministry apologized to the Parish Council but there was after all, 'a war on'. Compulsory purchase notices were served that winter and the bulldozers had rumbled into the village in

January 1942. Yet if those bulldozers were the unwelcome heralds of the twentieth century come to shatter Ansham's ancient peace, it was the arrival of the first Lancaster bombers that finally brought the war to the village. 647 Squadron was a new unit formed at Ansham Wolds in November 1942 that was declared 'operational' on 1st February, 1943.

Eleanor listened to the bombers climbing over Lincolnshire, wondered where they were off to tonight.

Sometimes she hated the bombers.

"Mummy, I can't sleep."

Eleanor smiled, her daughter Emily was calling to her from the top of the stairs and for a moment she forgot her worries and cast off her weariness. She got to her feet.

"I'm coming, darling!"

Chapter 3

Wednesday 22nd September, 1943
RAF Waltham Grange, Lincolnshire

Wing-Commander Adam Chantrey stood a little apart from the crowd as the first of *his* Lancasters lined-up for take-off. The pilot halted at the threshold, opened the throttles to zero boost against the brakes - checking for an even response – and then throttled back. Bomber Command was going to war and the same scenc was being enacted on tens of airfields from East Anglia to the Humber.

Adam huddled in his sheepskin flying jacket, lonely in his thoughts as the drizzle turned to rain. His Alsatian, Rufus, lay faithfully at his feet. The dog was as accustomed to the sound and fury of the Lancasters as his master for both were creatures of Bomber Command, living and moving in the twilight.

Droves of sightseers and well-wishers had gathered to see off 388 Squadron's heavies. The crowd was always bigger when the Lancasters were off to a distant target. Although few of the men and women in the crowd knew the identity of the target the fuel and bomb loads told their own tale. Tonight the Lancasters were loaded with sufficient fuel to strike deep into Germany, well beyond the bombed-out cities of the Ruhr Valley. The pulsating, rumbling thunder of Rolls Royce Merlin engines reverberated across the darkened fields. In the distance the big bombers rolled clumsily along the perimeter road like great dark spectres, navigation lights winking brightly in the gloom.

Q-Queenie's pilot advanced the throttles to zero boost against the brakes. This time he held the throttles open, waited for the Merlins to quicken and steady. Then he released the brakes. A desultory cheer went up: Q-Queenie was rolling.

At intervals of a minute or so her sisters followed, sweeping down the runway to unstick in a blur of power and spray. Adam watched his heavies departing, shivering. Sometimes it seemed as if the cold was eating into his soul; at twenty thousand feet over Germany there would be thirty degrees of frost in the cockpits of his Lancasters. He loathed staying behind. When he was flying there was no time for doubt. No time to get maudlin. Long after the last of his aircraft had departed and most of the well-wishers had noisily, cheerfully gone their many ways, he remained.

Alone.

All around Waltham Grange other airfields were sending off their heavies and the sky shook with the heartbeats of hundreds of Merlins straining for altitude. The Main Force was ascending the high road to Germany and the loneliness settled about him like a cloak. In around three hours from now high explosive bombs and bundles of stick incendiaries would begin to spill from the bellies of his heavies over Hanover.

Adam bent down to give Rufus a playful cuff.

"Come on, old man," he murmured, wandering back to his black, two-seater Bentley coupe. The omens seemed uniformly oppressive; ten-tenths cloud was predicted most of the way to the target, head winds on the way back, rain, and perhaps fog when the bombers landed. Rufus clambered into the car, muddying the seats with his soggy fur and paws.

Adam dropped behind the wheel, gunned the motor and set the car idling through the mist. Parking the Bentley behind the watchtower a few minutes later he returned the sentry's crisp salute and hurried inside with Rufus loping faithfully at his heels, making tracks down the broad concrete steps to the Operations Room in the basement bunker.

"Where have you been, my boy?" Boomed Group Captain Henderson, the Station

Commander, bending down to give Rufus a playful slap. "I was about to send out a search party. I half-suspected you'd hitched a lift to Hanover!"

It would not have been the first time Adam had defied a direct order to sit out an op to fly a raid as a passenger. But tonight was different. He had given the Old Man his word. Hitching a lift to Germany was *verboten*.

"No, sir. Not tonight," he replied, deadpan.

A smiling WAAF pushed a mug of cocoa into his cold hands. He was thankful that this particular WAAF spared him the star struck overlong look, or worse, the threat of a stifled girlish giggle. The ribbons of the DSO and DFC – Distinguished Service Order and the Distinguished Flying Cross – were faded, and the latter hardly uncommon on the Squadrons, but his notoriety, he refused to call it 'fame', had crept up upon him unawares over the last year like a night fighter on a moonless night. He had survived the Wilhelmshaven fiasco at the beginning of the war, a tour on Wellingtons, flown seventy ops on Blenheim night fighters, shot down four bombers, lived through two tours in command of Lancaster squadrons. He had earned the right to be 'notorious', although oddly, it gave him little or no satisfaction for it was in his nature to much rather have been anonymous.

Group Captain Henderson got up, thumped the taller, younger man on the back. "Still raining?"

"Yes, sir." The Old Man's indefatigable good humour jarred Adam's nerves. "Everybody got off okay," he added, sniffing.

He felt less than well, as if he was sickening for something.

Chapter 4

Wednesday 22nd September, 1943
RAF Ansham Wolds, Lincolnshire

Aircraftwoman Suzy Mills had driven the Station Master, Group Captain Alexander, out to see off his beloved heavies. She stood at the runway's edge watching 647 Squadron's Lancasters roaring into the night; the thunder of Merlins was deafening as the heavily laden aircraft struggled to get into the air. Suzy longed to cheer and wave like the others but she never did. It seemed wrong, somehow. When the Squadron went to war she was invariably struck by how unbearably sad it all was. The courage of the crews made her feel humble. They were so brave. Brave beyond her comprehension and yet sometimes, it seemed such a terrible, terrible waste.

When the last Lancaster's navigation lights winked out in the darkness the Station Master walked slowly, stiffly back to the car. He was lost in his premonitions, weariness etched deep in his craggy features. The tiredness slowed his movements and clouded his eyes. They said the Old Man took everything to heart. They said that some nights he could hardly bear to send out the crews. At first Suzy had wondered if the other girls were pulling her leg but not now. Tonight, her passenger seemed resigned, beaten down, old. Old and bowed as if pressed down by some invisible, crushing mill stone.

Suzy held the door open.

"Ops Room, please, my dear," directed the Station Master, forcing a semblance of a smile before he slumped into the back seat.

"Yes, sir."

Suzy had been Group Captain Alexander's driver for most of the four months she had been at Ansham Wolds. The other girls teased her unmercifully about her finishing school manners and her 'airs and graces', the self-same qualifications which had persuaded her Section Officer to assign her as the Station Commander's driver. She could live with the sniping, she was free of her family and she was doing something useful at last. That was what mattered. To be doing something useful. To be doing one's bit.

"We shall be making an early start tomorrow morning," Alexander announced, quietly. "The Wingco and I have an appointment at Group Headquarters at oh-nine hundred hours. We'll have to leave the station around oh-eight-hundred."

"Yes, sir."

Suzy concentrated on the road. A darkened aerodrome was a dangerous place even when the Squadron was airborne. The Old Man spoke distantly, as if his thoughts were faraway, flying into the unknown with his Lancasters.

"Yes, an early start, I'm afraid," he sighed. "Can't be helped. Wouldn't do to keep the AOC waiting, would it, now?"

"No, sir," Suzy agreed, earnestly.

Alexander chuckled, softly. "No, sir," he echoed, gently teasing.

She knew that there was no harm in it because there was something altogether reassuring about the Old Man, something fatherly, something wholly lacking in malice. The windscreen wipers struggled as the rain suddenly lashed down.

"Filthy old night," observed her passenger.

Suzy peered through the blackness. "Horrible, sir."

The worst of the squall had passed by the time she parked the car in front of the watchtower and jumped out to open the door for her passenger. As the Station Master stepped out of the car the Adjutant, normally the most measured, phlegmatic of men, bustled up to him, breathless.

"There's a problem, sir," he gasped. "One of our Lancs is in trouble. R-Robert. Engine fire, we think."

"Dicey," Alexander remarked, gruffly,

heading straight inside without a backward glance. It suddenly began to rain, again. A hard, cold rain.

Suzy sat in the car for several minutes waiting for the downpour to relent long enough for her to garage the vehicle and to get back to the Waafery without getting soaked. However, as she waited another idea took root. Although she was supposed to book the car back into the pool without delay, she hated the thought of missing any excitement. At the bidding of the Senior WAAF, a forbidding maternal presence, she always carried a thermos of freshly made cocoa for the Old Man. 'The Station Master may be the finest gentleman in Bomber Command,' Squadron Officer Laing had told Suzy, very sternly, 'however, since he has no care for his own health *we* must!' Possession of the thermos of cocoa now provided Suzy with a pretext, albeit flimsy, to linger. Clutching the thermos she cautiously ascended the narrow steps to the crowded watchtower balcony.

The rain turned to a spotting drizzle as the latest squall blew over.

647 Squadron's senior officers were in a huddle and nobody noticed her. Guiltily, she edged into the shadows. Group Captain Alexander was talking with the duty controller. He had cast off his tiredness, taken command.

His voice boomed into the night.

"Well, do we know if R-Robert managed to jettison, or not?"

"No, sir. We're having trouble raising them. All we know is that they've got engine trouble and that they're heading back."

The bombing leader, a four-square, jovial man put down his pipe for a moment and leaned nonchalantly on the railing. "Unlikely to have had a chance to jettison, sir."

Suzy could tell the Old Man was angry. Really angry. She could feel him scowling. She shrank into the shadows. Everybody knew the bombing leader was something of a buffoon. 'All stuffed shirt and bluster', she had overhead one old lag complain.

"Very unlikely," continued the bombing leader, a portrait in detachment. "Hasn't been airborne long enough to reach a safe altitude."

"Damn! What's R-Robert got onboard tonight?"

"A cookie, a couple of thousand pounders and ten SBCs." The bombing leader scratched his scalp. "Oh, and a five hundred pounder. For luck, what!"

Since she had been at Ansham Wolds Suzy had received a thorough grounding in the deadly lexicon of the bombing war. A 'cookie' was a two-ton high explosive blast bomb - a so-called 'blockbuster' - an awesome weapon that knocked down whole streets. 'SBCs' were Special Bomb Containers – coffin-like rectangular canisters - into which could be packed up to ninety four-pounder thermite and magnesium stick incendiaries. R-Robert would have taken off with approximately one-and-a-half tons of these dreadful firebombs in her belly, each primed to spontaneously ignite on exposure to the atmosphere and to explode on contact with water. She shuddered. In a big raid, cookies dropped in their hundreds shattered whole neighbourhoods, ripped off thousands of roofs and put out countless windows. Thereafter, hundreds of thousands of incendiaries rained into the wreckage because the plan – every night without exception - was to set whole cities ablaze like giant funeral pyres.

"An extra five hundred pounder?" Group Captain Alexander growled dangerously. "For luck?"

"Absolutely, sir."

"Who authorised that?"

The bombing leader straightened, belatedly becoming aware of the grimness of the Station Master's tone.

"Er, the Wingco, sir."

"Did he indeed!"

"Yes, sir. An extra five hundred pounder fused long delay with a mark twenty-seven pistol, sir."

A bomb fused to go off long after the raid was over. A bomb intended to kill people returning to their homes, or to blow up while the Germans were attempting to defuse it. Suzy shuddered. Although she understood it was part and parcel of the bombing, and that they were fighting a brutal and ruthless enemy who was playing exactly the same deadly, cruel, vicious game, it was still unspeakable.

The Old Man glared at the bombing leader for a moment. "Who's flying R-Robert?" He barked, irascibly.

"Witherspoon," somebody offered.

"He's new, isn't he?" This from the Adjutant.

"Second op, I think. He borrowed Peter Tilliard's crew for tonight's show," somebody added.

Suzy could not place the sprog pilot's face. However, she had no problem picturing Flight-Lieutenant Tilliard. He was tall, nearly six feet, fair, good looking, handsome but not in a brash sort of way. He had very nice eyes; he was quite dishy, really, she thought. Gossip in the Waafery said the Wingco had it in for him. It was also said he did not drink - odd among aircrew - and that he kept to himself. His aircraft had been attacked by a night fighter coming back from Mannheim a fortnight ago and was still on the sick list recovering from the injuries he had suffered that night. A gunner had been killed and in the confusion of the attack his bomb-aimer had baled out. The other girls said the bomb-aimer must have been 'temporarily insane'; but that was what everybody always said when some poor boy panicked and baled out without orders. Tilliard had flown back from Germany on two engines and crash-landed at Manston in Kent.

The flare path lights blazed into life.

An icy hand clutched Suzy's heart when she saw the Lancaster. R-Robert was dragging a long streamer of crimson flame across the pitch black canopy of the heavens.

"Somebody find Wing-Commander Fulshawe!" Called Group Captain Alexander.

"He seems to have vanished, sir," replied the Adjutant, apologetically.

"He should be here!"

Suzy gazed spellbound as the drama rushed towards its dreadful conclusion. The clamour of the Lancaster's de-synchronized Merlins provided a hideous overture to what followed. R-Robert glided down the centre-line of the runway and briefly, tantalizingly, it seemed as if all would be well. Then the Lancaster slewed to the left. The bomber's nose dipped. The onlookers heard the pulse of her Merlins quicken as the pilot opened the throttles in one last hopeless attempt to defy gravity.

It was too late.

R-Robert stalled and death came quickly, fierily in the night.

The Lancaster's port wing fell away into space, struck the ground, dug into the mud and thirty tons of bomber, high explosives, incendiaries and 100-octane petrol cart-wheeled to ruin. The huge orange fireball tumbled across the airfield as R-Robert disintegrated into a thousand fractured pieces, each engulfed by licking, consuming flames. The tail section of the bomber separated from the rest of the fuselage at the first impact, the port wing crumpled and shattered. One Merlin, still running, hurtled clear of the fireball and imbedded itself in the mire of the infield. Afterwards, there was only the roaring of the flames and the glowing silence; that terrible silence that followed every big crash.

"Oh, my god!"

"Poor clots!"

Suzy stared into the brightly flickering middle distance. She listened as the controller shouted a string of orders. He was determined to halt the headlong rush of the fire tenders and ambulances towards the burning wreckage. Until she got to Ansham Wolds Suzy had assumed an operational airfield ran like clockwork; like a well-oiled, efficient machine. In reality the station ran not so much like a well-oiled machine, as a lunatic asylum in the hands of its inmates. Bedlam. Utter bedlam. And never was this truer than when there was a flap. At Ansham Wolds she had learned very quickly that crashes brought out both the very best and the very worst in people.

"I don't care if you can walk on water, old boy," remonstrated the duty controller, acidly. "You can jolly well stay where you are until we find out if R-Robert's cookie is still under that lot!"

"We have debris blocking the main runway," reported a voice from within the watch tower. The runway lights had blinked off. "Hell! We've just lost the flare path."

"I can see that!" Snorted Group Captain Alexander.

The fires on the field cast a ghostly light into the faces of the men and women on the balcony. Suzy felt sick. She invariably felt sick when she saw an aircraft crash and burn. Lancasters, Halifaxes, Stirlings or Wellingtons, *all* bombers burned when they crashed. She had witnessed her first big crash within forty-eight hours of arriving at Ansham Wolds; coming into land in broad daylight after a routine flight test a Lancaster had, for no apparent reason, fallen out of the sky and blown up in a field several hundred yards short of the runway. A great plume of smoke had climbed into the clear blue of that otherwise perfect summer afternoon. Later they had identified nine bodies in the wreckage, seven crew members including the Squadron's second-in-command, and two 'joyriding' WAAFs.

The bombing leader was studying the wreckage through binoculars. "Maybe they jettisoned their cookie after all," he offered. "A crash like that usually sets off a cookie."

This prompted solemn nods of agreement but the Station Master was unconvinced.

"We shall see."

"Well," said the bombing leader, dispassionately, "if there's a cookie under that lot it's liable to brew up pretty soon. Right now it'll be baking nicely, what?"

"Perhaps, sightseers ought to be ordered down to the shelters?" Suggested the Adjutant. "Until we know what's happened to R's cookie?"

The bombing leader scoffed at this. "Don't be wet, old boy!"

The Old Man coughed. "Better safe than sorry," he said, turning to the Adjutant. "Get it organised, please."

In a daze Suzy unscrewed the lid of the

Station Master's thermos and with trembling hands poured out a mug of cocoa.

"Cocoa, sir," she asked, stepping out of the shadows.

Alexander recognised her, grimaced.

"Thank you, my dear. I'm glad somebody's on the ball around..."

He never finished his sentence. The livid, blinding flash of R-Robert's cookie coming to the boil erupted in the night with a sudden, unimaginable ferocity. Momentarily, the Station Master was silhouetted against the pure white light of the explosion. In the coal-cellar blackness that followed, the murderous, rumbling crump of the huge detonation rampaged across the aerodrome like a hurricane. Splintered glass, cries of pain, screams of alarm filled the air as the blast wave rolled past into the night.

Suzy instinctively flung her arms in front of her face, twisting away from the flash. In so doing she slipped on the damp metal floor, lost her balance and fell backwards. Had it not been for the restraining arms of the stocky man in flying sheepskins standing directly behind her she would have ended up in a heap on the floor, or worse, tumbled straight down the steps to the tarmac twenty feet below. The contents of both the flask and the mug caught the man full in the chest.

"I'm so sorry, I..."

Shards of glass crunched underfoot. Muted groans and curses emerged from the inner recesses of the tower. In the background the racket of fire engines racing to douse R-Robert's widely scattered incendiaries was unnaturally raucous.

"I'm sorry, sir," she apologised, making as if to dab at his cocoa-wet chest.

"No matter," Wing-Commander Fulshawe muttered. Everybody turned and stared at the Squadron Commander. The fires on the field reflected dully in the tears trickling down his ruddy cheeks. "No matter..."

Chapter 5

Thursday 23rd September, 1943
RAF Waltham Grange, Lincolnshire

The clock on the wall told Adam Chantrey that the Main Force was bombing Hanover. His office was dim and cold and he was alone, thinking of other nights. Other nights like this night. Many, many other nights spent in the frozen wasteland of the heavens far from home.

The Main Force was fire-razing over Germany; the roar of Merlins raged in his ears, shook him until his senses reeled. The white hot dazzle of searchlights groping for prey four miles high seared his eyes, flak erupted in the distance. His Lancaster lurched drunkenly across the swirling slipstream of another unseen heavy up ahead, soared wildly a moment later as her bombs tumbled down into the maelstrom. Below him another city was burning. He remembered Hamburg burning. He would never forget the fires of Hamburg because some things were with a man forever. There could be no more terrible thing than a great city burning, to see the crimson hearts of hundreds of huge fires raging out of control beneath the clouds; clouds painted like mile upon mile of blood-soaked cotton wool...

"Tea, sir," prompted the plump WAAF, bleary-eyed. "Adjutant's orders, sir," she explained, apologetically.

Rufus, dozing in front of the desk, stirred.

"Thanks, just put it down." Adam smiled and the WAAF blushed. After the woman was gone he wondered if she had somebody flying tonight. Somebody she cared for, or loved or who perhaps, cared for her, too. He hoped not.

Lighting a cigarette, he gazed for a while at his battered silver cigarette case. A present from Helen Fulshawe in those days when they were innocents, reckless to the point of folly and he had loved her more it seemed than life itself.

'Carry it with you always, darling,' Helen had asked. 'Let it be your lucky charm. And promise me that every time it brings you back safe, you'll think of me.' He had promised it. And true to his word every time it brought him back safely, he thought of her. Even now.

He shut his eyes.

Helen was the wife of the finest, bravest fellow he had ever known. Bert Fulshawe had 647 Squadron at Ansham Wolds, some thirty miles north of Waltham Grange. Bert and he were both overdue a rest. For Adam the axe had already fallen, he was grounded pending posting. No doubt, Bert's turn would not be long delayed. The last time they had met - a fortnight ago at one of the AOC's regular conferences at Group Headquarters - Bert had seemed tired and a little jaded. Typically, he had complained of a head cold and brushed off Adam's concern. He had not thought overmuch about it, everybody was entitled to an off day in this business.

Helen. Oh, Helen...

The first wave would be turning for home, now. The minutes dragged by.

"Still up, then?" The voice of Adam's long-suffering navigator, and 388 Squadron's Senior Navigation Officer, Squadron Leader Ben Hardiman, broke into his brooding.

"So it would seem," he scowled.

Ben had known Adam too long to pay heed to this moodiness. He sauntered in and slumped in the nearest chair, leaning down to pat Rufus on the rump as he settled.

"I'll go then."

"No, don't mind me. Feeling sorry for myself, that's all."

Ben said nothing and a quietness fell between them. Above the newcomer Sopwith Pups diced with the multi-coloured Fokker Triplanes of the Richthofen Circus in a series of fading prints hung across the clammy end wall of the Nissen hut. The pictures had belonged to Adam's predecessor. They came with the office and the Squadron. The previous Wingco had been a keen type. A Hun-hater through and through. The genuine article, if ever such a thing existed. Neither Adam nor his Navigation Leader had ever met the fellow and they probably never would, given that the poor chap had gone for a burton over Krefeld in June. Careless. Very careless.

"Something on your mind, Ben?"

Ben Hardiman was a big man; and he shifted his bear-like frame uneasily in the chair.

"In a manner of speaking," he confessed, clasping his large, scarred hands before him.

Adam waited patiently, silent. They were friends, often of the distant kind but the firmest, unshakable friends for all that. They had flown together nearly three years but it had made them hard, shy of speaking their minds. It was as if they both understood that most of the things which really mattered were best left unsaid. It was the sort of pact a man broke at his own risk. They were closer than brothers, yet sometimes strangers.

"I know nothing's been said," Ben murmured, "but you've been *screened*. Right?"

Adam nodded. He and Ben had met in November 1940, thrown together on Bristol Blenheim night fighters at Marwood Lodge, in Wiltshire. Ben was a sergeant navigator and radar operator marked out from his fellows by the brand new ribbon of the DFM - the Distinguished Flying Medal, the non-commissioned man's equivalent of the Distinguished Flying Cross - worn nonchalantly on the left breast of his tunic. Many DFCs were awarded, few DFMs, and each was hard won. Ben had earned his Distinguished Flying medal dragging men from the burning wreck of a crashed Blenheim and he would bear the scars of that day to his grave.

'This job's a waste of bloody time!' Adam's first CO at Marwood Lodge - the hollow-eyed survivor of a dozen do or die low-level raids against German invasion barges - had complained.

Notwithstanding, Adam was itching to try his hand at the new, mysterious art of night fighting and was in no mood to be disheartened. Fighter Command had driven the Luftwaffe from the skies by day so the Heinkels, Junkers and Dorniers had switched to night bombing. The London Blitz was two months old and Marwood Lodge's Blenheims had been hastily converted from day bombers to night fighters. Night fighting turned out to be a dangerous game. A fortnight later his hollow-eyed CO flew into a hillside, and it was three long months before anybody at Marwood Lodge successfully intercepted and shot down an enemy bomber.

'Really, sir?' Adam had asked his new CO that first day at Marwood Lodge.

'Complete waste of time. Still, you'll need a navigator, I suppose,' his CO had sighed, wearily. 'You're a damned fool to volunteer for this lark but I've got just the chap for you. You'll get on famously. He's mad, too!'

'DFC, skipper?' Ben had observed amiably.

'Wilhelmshaven,' Adam had replied, evenly.

The big man had raised an eyebrow. 'Hairy show, they say?'

Adam had shrugged.

'Oh, I wouldn't say that. You don't want to believe everything you hear. DFM, I see?'

'Bad landing coming back from Boulogne,' Ben shrugged.

'I try to avoid bad landings, personally.'

They had exchanged mutual looks of guarded respect. 'We'll get on fine then, skipper.'

Adam often thought about those days in Wiltshire. Night after night chasing shadows in the darkness over southern England slowly learning the night fighting trade. It was trial and error, mostly error but eventually they had learned what they were about, and somehow, survived long enough to draw blood. Watching a German bomber - a Heinkel 111 – fall and dash itself into a flaming ruin on the Downs near Alresford, east of Winchester, had been the crowning glory. The next morning they had driven across country and inspected the scorched ground. The Home Guard had cordoned off the field. The broken, charred bodies of the Heinkel's crew lay in five, contorted heaps on the wet ground. Crows picked and flies had settled on the corpses, nobody cared.

So much for glory.

"The new Wingco's due down next week. Solid fellow, so I'm told." Adam said, relieved to get the news off his chest. "The crew is screened. I'd planned to fill you in tomorrow."

"No idea what postings are in the offing, I suppose?"

"Nothing officially, I'm afraid."

"What about unofficially?"

"Unofficially..."

The shrill ringing of the phone on Adam's desk cut him off. Unofficially, they were both on their way to Operational Training Units: Ben to Lichfield as Chief Navigation Instructor, Adam to take command at Little Marsham, in Shropshire.

"Chantrey," he said, snatching up the receiver. He listened intently. "Oh-nine-thirty hours. At Group. Thank you, sir." He replaced the phone on its cradle and looked to his friend. "That was the Station Master. I'm to report to the AOC tomorrow morning."

Ben knew better than to ask what was going on.

Adam was reading his thoughts.

"Sorry, the Old Man didn't give anything away."

"No." Ben's good humour had suddenly been replaced by a dull, nagging foreboding. "Oh well, I think I'll put my head down."

Chapter 6

Thursday 23rd September, 1943
No. 1 Group Headquarters, Bawtry Hall, South Yorkshire

Group Headquarters was a rambling old country house off the Doncaster Road. A shanty town of Nissen huts had sprouted in its grounds, unsightly wartime appendages to the ivy-clad grand mansion of a former age.

It was raining hard as Adam parked the Bentley and hurried inside. All his Lancasters had returned from Hanover; one aircraft had been struck by incendiaries over the target and flown home on three Merlins, and two others bore flak marks.

His crews were safe.

However, having sat through the debriefings he had formed his own, less than sanguine conclusions about the success of the night's work. Visibility over the target had been good and the bombing, particularly in the early stages of the attack, concentrated. Unfortunately, there was one rather big fly in the ointment. Several of his old lags reported the winds over Hanover were much stronger than predicted. In itself, this should not have caused the raid to miscarry but Adam strongly suspected the Pathfinders' initial ground marking and the bulk of the first wave's bombs had gone down at least two, and possibly as many as four to five miles, south of the intended aiming point in the city centre. Thereafter, the bombing effort would have tended to creep back further and further away from the city; if he was right most of the bomb loads dropped in what 388 Squadron's Intelligence Officer euphemistically termed the 'target area', had probably fallen on open country.

Too many raids were going off half-cock and this morning he was ready, willing and angry enough to tell the Group Commander as much. He had nothing to lose and the opportunity to beard the AOC in his lair was too good to miss. It was high time somebody made a scene.

Reporting to the WAAF in the oak-beamed ante-room, he was a little surprised to be immediately ushered into the presence of the great man. The AOC was sitting behind his desk and Adam discovered that he was not his only visitor. Group Captain Alexander, Bert Fulshawe's Station Commander at Ansham Wolds, rose to greet him. The two men had met several times, in passing. Bert always spoke highly of Alexander and in Adam's book there was no finer recommendation.

"How do you do, sir."

"Good to see you again, Chantrey."

Adam shook the older man's hand, noted the gravitas in his voice. Instantly, he was on his guard. Something was wrong. Very wrong. The AOC got to his feet, came forward. Adam straightened and saluted.

"My congratulations on the Bar to your DSO, Chantrey. It was well-deserved." The Group Commander's stare rifled into the younger man's eyes as he shook his hand. His voice was quiet, razor-edged. When he asked a question he deployed words like a surgeon wielding a scalpel, cutting clinically, precisely, ruthlessly to the heart of a thing. His cold, aloof manner intimidated his peers, and terrorized most of his subordinates.

But not Adam Chantrey.

"Thank you, sir."

The AOC stepped back. "I'm told the Pathfinders let us down again last night?"

"No, sir."

The older man raised an eyebrow.

"No? Then, perhaps you'd care to tell me exactly what did go wrong?"

Adam steadied himself. He was fighting the Luftwaffe, not 8 Group. Not even when the Pathfinders got the winds wrong and put down their TIs – Target Indicators - in a field several miles from anywhere. It was no picnic over Germany. These things happened and continual sniping did not help.

"My understanding," the AOC went on. "Is that 8 Group put their initial red spot markers down at least three miles south of the aiming point."

"The crosswinds were stronger than forecast," Adam returned, evenly. 8 Group's problems were not unique they were simply the problems of the Main Force writ large for everybody to see. "If there had been a master of ceremonies on hand he would have been able to correct for the wind error as the raid progressed. In the absence of a Master Bomber the Pathfinders did the best they could in the circumstances, sir."

"In your opinion?"

Adam reminded himself that it was his resolve, rather than his grasp of tactics that was under the microscope. Inter-group rivalry was never less than fierce, often it was bitter, exacerbated by the simmering antipathy which existed between several of the Main Force bomber barons and Don Bennett, the flamboyant, and to his older peers, infuriatingly youthful commander of the Pathfinder Force. Bennett of course, unlike the other Group Commanders had actually flown ops in *this* war.

"Until we adopt more flexible tactics," he said, snatching up the gauntlet. "More fiascos like last night's are inevitable and we shall go on wasting aircraft and crews to no good purpose, sir. In my opinion, sir."

The AOC was Adam's height, his features haughty, nose aquiline, eyes clear, steely blue. An austere, cerebral man he sometimes seemed out of place in the company of his fellow Group Commanders.

He looked into the younger man's eyes, nodded imperceptibly.

"Possibly," he said. "Possibly." Then inexplicably, his countenance softened. He had not expected the younger man to yield and would have been disappointed, profoundly disappointed if he had. Men like Adam Chantrey were a breed apart. Men like Chantrey enjoyed a special standing among their contemporaries. Men like Chantrey were a law unto themselves, loose cannons. Men like Chantrey had walked through the Vale of the Shadow countless times and against all the odds, they had survived. The normal rules simply did not apply to men like Adam Chantrey.

"Sit down, gentlemen," he directed, resuming his seat behind the big, polished desk under the window. "I'll come straight to the point, Chantrey," he prefaced, while Adam and Group Captain Alexander settled. "So far as I'm concerned you've finished your tour.

You've done a fine job at Waltham Grange. You're entitled to a rest. However, something has come up, and circumstances oblige me to ask you if you are prepared to continue flying operations. For the time being at least."

Adam swallowed hard. When he spoke he hardly knew his own voice. It never occurred to him to say: "No!" Not for a single moment.

"Count me in, sir."

"Good, I thought that's what you'd say." The AOC regarded the young Wing-Commander distantly, dispassionately for a moment. "Alex will fill you in in due course but they've had a bit of a bad run at Ansham Wolds."

Adam stiffened. Everything came into sharp focus: Alexander's presence and the unexpected summons to Bawtry Hall.

"I don't have to spell it out for a chap like you," the AOC continued. Nevertheless, for reasons best known to himself he did spell 'it' out. "Bad luck at the wrong time, high chop-rate, not enough experienced crews making it through a tour. Happened before and it'll happen again. Nothing to be gained by dwelling on spilt milk. The important thing is what we do now."

Alexander shifted uneasily in his chair.

Adam was oblivious to his discomfort.

Oh, no. Not Bert, too. Not Bert. Not Bert

Fulshawe: my Flight Commander, mentor, protector and friend on Wellingtons at Faldwell a lifetime ago.

"Alex needs somebody to step in and sort things out," the Group Commander was saying. "Somebody to put the Squadron back on an even keel, as it were."

"Dead man's shoes, and all that guff," Adam said to himself. His thoughts were suddenly far away, transported back in time. Back nearly four years to that fateful week before the first Christmas of the war when he was Bert Fulshawe's second pilot on the Wilhelmshaven disaster. God in Heaven, they had been such innocents abroad that day! Swanning around off the German coast with no fighter escort on the off chance of finding a pocket battleship to bomb! What manner of madness was that? 'Phoney War!' It had seemed like a game until then. Just a stupid game. In those days nobody countenanced bombing anything other than out and out 'military' targets. Dropping bombs on civilians - shock and horror - even accidentally, was actually a court-martial offence.

It had been such a beautiful, clear, sunny winter day: perfect flying weather. The force of twenty-four Wellingtons drawn from four squadrons had droned east in a stately gaggle high above the grey-green North Sea. Two aircraft - the lucky two – had turned back early because of mechanical problems. The damned, the remaining twenty-two, had pressed on. Over Wilhelmshaven there was no sign of a pocket battleship and in that bizarre lost age of innocence nobody questioned aimlessly stooging around for over an hour, in full view of the enemy coast looking for something suitably 'naval' to bomb. It was sheer lunacy. Eventually, stumbling upon a flotilla of small warships the formation had bombed from high altitude.

It was just like a training flight until the Luftwaffe had come out to play.

There was no panic. Not at first. Excitement, anticipation, a queasiness in the pit of the stomach, but no panic. They had climbed higher, tightened formation, waited for the fighters to come within range of their combined battery of 132 Browning machine guns. H-E-I-G-H-T spelled S-A-F-E-T-Y even in those days of 'phoney war' and in their naivety the men in the Wellingtons had trusted to height and to their concentrated defensive firepower to keep the Bosch at bay.

They were mistaken.

Horribly mistaken.

There was nothing remotely 'phoney' about the war that December afternoon. Ugly, snub-nosed, single-engine Me109s arrived first:

tiny, fast-moving specks low on the horizon swarming up to investigate the big, clumsy bombers. From afar they were like wasps swarming to defend a violated nest. Everybody expected the fighters to form up, gather themselves for the assault. Instead, the fighters attacked immediately, hurtling in from all angles, guns-blazing as they flashed past. The leading Wellington was knocked off station, port engine smoking in the first pass. Inexorably, it lost altitude and slowly fell behind. In the blink of an eye a dozen fighters fell on it. Three more Wellingtons went down in as many minutes. Time and again the red and yellow-nosed fighters barrelled through the formation, in twos and fours, contemptuous of the Brownings. The clatter of gunfire was continuous, the cockpit filled with the stench of burnt cordite, spent cartridge cases cascaded out of the turrets, spilled impotently into space.

The first phase of the battle only lasted ten minutes.

Without warning, the boys in the 109s disengaged and briefly it seemed the worst was over. But that was when the real nightmare began. The 109s had just been the hors d'oeuvre, next came the main course. A pack of twin-engine Me110s had caught up with the battle. Unlike the fleeter, lighter-gunned

Me109s the big, cannon-armed 110s had no need to shoot it out at close quarters. With almost painstaking deliberation they took up station above and slightly behind the formation and commenced a withering fire from well outside the range of the Wellingtons' puny, rifle-calibre Brownings. One by one bombers smoked, burned and tumbled. Parachutes opened and swayed above the cold North Sea as bomber after bomber succumbed. The 110s took it in turns to batter a bomber out of the formation, the marauding 109s gathered around each successive straggler like a pack of starving wolves and tore it to pieces. There was no respite. No mercy. No quarter. It was pure bloody murder.

'My word. These chaps are very, very good,' Bert Fulshawe observed. At the height of the battle he had jovially explained, at great length, to his terrified second pilot about his aged, spinster Aunt Phoebe and her thatched cottage in Gloucestershire, whence he had recently despatched Helen and his baby son and heir, Jack. Helen was on a pedestal, a Flight Commander's wife, distant, untouchable. Bert seemed oblivious to the battle, only occasionally breaking off from extolling the virtues of Rose Cottage, or the village of Moorehampstead, or Helen's cooking to remark on the exemplary airmanship and the dubious ancestry of their foes.

'Bastards!'

The carnage went on and on and on until only eleven Wellingtons remained and most of the fighters had either exhausted their ammunition or were running low on fuel. As dusk descended G-George was the last Wellington to be shot down. Adam watched the cannon fire smashing into G-George. Repeated strikes ripped off the starboard engine nacelle. Fragments of aileron, flap and wing disintegrated and crashed back into R-Robert. As if in slow motion G-George shuddered as the next burst chewed up and spat out huge chunks of fuselage. One second G-George was taking punishment, the next it exploded, disintegrated in mid-air and R-Robert was flying through the wreckage.

There was no smoke.

No fire.

G-George just blew up.

Bert was pontificating on cricket, recounting his vivid recollections of an innings he had seen the Australian maestro Don Bradman play against one of the Universities, Cambridge or Oxford. Adam could not recall which. 'Footwork, that's the key,' Bert maintained. 'Never seen a chap so nimble on his feet. Didn't matter where they bowled at him...'

That was when something hit the glass panel in front of the first pilot's seat, smashed through it and thudded, sickeningly into the main spar behind the cockpit, neatly decapitating the navigator on the way. The slipstream thundered into the aircraft through the gaping hole, swirled like a blizzard into the fuselage.

'Must have had a five hundred pounder hang up!' Bert shouted, blood filling his eyes.

Adam was paralysed, rigid with fear, helpless. It had never happened to him before, and never since. But that day he went to pieces, clung petrified to the controls, staring blindly, wildly into the empty sky where G-George had been. Bert was in a bad way but he knew his second pilot had frozen. He punched Adam's shoulder and when this failed to bring him to his senses, had thrown a second blow at his head.

Adam looked dazedly at Fulshawe's bloodied countenance.

'Be a good chap,' Bert had yelled, 'do your best to get us back...'

Now Bert was gone.

"Oh, God!" Adam cried, privately.

The AOC's voice brought him back to the present. "I'm considering pulling 647 Squadron out of the line for the time being. What's your feeling, Alex?"

"I believe it would be counter-productive, sir."

It was this that snapped Adam out of his brooding. He had no intention of respectfully waiting to be asked whether he had a view on the subject. Particularly, as it was a subject on which he had extremely strong views and he was uniquely qualified to comment.

"I agree with Group Captain Alexander, sir," he declared, laconically.

"Do you, indeed!"

"Yes, sir. In my experience it's often better for a Squadron that's been having a bad trot to carry on operating, even at a reduced level, than to single it out for special treatment."

The Group Commander's scrutiny was intense.

Adam did not flinch from it.

"It's a question of morale, sir. The chaps need to know that somebody, somewhere believes in them. You can't turn a bad run around by sitting on the ground. You have to carry on flying ops."

The AOC turned to Alexander. "Very good. 647 Squadron will remain on the order of battle. However, the Squadron will operate at flight strength until further notice."

"Yes, sir."

The AOC turned to the younger man, dismissed him. "Thank you, Chantrey. That will be all. Would you wait outside please? Group Captain Alexander will join you shortly."

Adam got up, saluted and left.

Alexander soon emerged from the AOC's office and suggested that before they went their separate ways, they should have a chat over a cup of tea in the Mess.

"Break the ice, so to speak."

"Capital idea, sir," Adam agreed.

Neither man said another word until they were both settled in armchairs by the window.

"You were on Wimpeys with Bert Fulshawe," the older man said.

"Yes, sir."

"He was a good man."

"Do we know what happened, sir?"

Alexander stared past him across the rain swept parkland beyond the high bay windows of the alcove in which they sat. Momentarily, his thoughts seemed lost in the grey, autumnal morning.

"Oh, yes," he confirmed, sadly. He dug his pipe out of one pocket and his tobacco pouch from another. "I'm aware that you and Bert were close. He often spoke of you. Very highly, needless to say."

Adam said nothing. He lit a cigarette as the older man packed the bowl of his pipe.

"Like yourself, Bert was screened last week.

He was waiting for his posting to come through." Alexander continued, wearily. His voice was pitched low. "Between you and I; Bert was pretty much at the end of his tether and he badly needed a rest. Of course, he wouldn't have any of it. But that's by the by."

Adam listened patiently, sipping tea and smoking his cigarette.

"Anyway. Last night we had three crews abort just before the off. Bert hared out to the dispersals. By all accounts he completely lost his rag with one of the pilots. From what I can gather the pilot, a sprog by the name of Witherspoon, reported a mag drop on his port inner. Bert gave him a frightful dressing down in front of the ground crew and ordered him to take his kite up. Thirty minutes later Witherspoon's aircraft crashed attempting to land back at Ansham. He had an engine fire. The whole crew was killed. Poor Bert was beside himself. I tried to talk him round. I got a couple of stiff drinks down him, told him to forget about it. He'd only done what he thought was right."

"A chap's entitled to lose his rag once in a while."

"Absolutely."

There was an awkward silence. Adam broke it.

"Then what happened, sir?"

The Group Captain puffed on his pipe, looked up and met his eye.

"Bert went back to his room." There was a moment's hesitation. "Got out his service revolver and blew out his brains."

"I see." Adam turned off his emotions, stubbed out his cigarette. He knew he ought to feel something but he was numb. Later he would mourn his friend but right here and now he could feel nothing. It was an aircrew reflex. An old lag's best last defence when something unspeakable had happened. "Messy. If you don't mind me asking, will you be corresponding with Bert's wife, sir?"

Alexander put down his pipe.

"Yes. It's damned awkward, though."

"Quite so, sir."

"The AOC's keen to keep this thing in the family, as it were. He doesn't feel there's any need for the details to become widely known. I'm sure you agree. The official telegram will say that Bert was killed in a flying accident."

"Oh." Adam tried not to sound too unenthusiastic. In his experience, these things usually came out in the wash, sooner or later.

"A crash."

"I see."

Group Captain Alexander sat forward. He was as ill at ease as the younger man and decided to change the subject. "The AOC wants you to assume command of 647 Squadron on Saturday. Does that give you enough time to straighten things out at Waltham Grange?"

"Yes, sir."

"Will you be bringing your own crew with you?"

"I don't know, sir. That's something I'll have to give some thought to."

The two men parted shortly afterwards. A curt handshake at the door of the Mess and Adam was walking back to the Bentley. Rufus woke up when he dropped behind the wheel.

"Hello, old chap," he chuckled. "How'd you fancy a new home." The Alsatian wagged his tail violently, licked his master's face until Adam fended him off. "Poor old Uncle Bertie, what?" He engaged reverse gear and manoeuvred the car out onto the road. Once past the guards at the gate he sent the Bentley roaring south, down the Lincoln Road at his customary breakneck speed. "Poor Bert..."

If the Wilhelmshaven debacle had taught Adam anything it was that it was better for everybody if you could somehow set grief aside, file it away in some darkened recess of the mind and concentrate on the business of living.

"Who is that happy warrior that we should

all wish to be?"

He used to think it was Bert Fulshawe, D.S.O., DFC, born 9 June, 1911 - died 22 September, 1943, beloved husband of Helen and doting father of six year old Jack and two year old Kate.

Had anybody told Helen, yet?

Helen Ledbetter had been, by a country mile, the prettiest girl at Faldwell. Flaxen-haired, leggy with sparkling blue eyes Helen was the eldest daughter of a local Magistrate, gentleman farmer and the Faldwell Hunt's master of hounds. Bert had courted her with a dogged determination, learned to ride so he could ride out with the hounds, disregarding spills and rebuffs aplenty before winning her over and dragging her to the altar. Helen had never really forgiven Bert for sending her off 'into exile' with Aunt Phoebe in Gloucestershire at the outbreak of hostilities. She and the old lady were like chalk and cheese, had never hit it off. Cut off from her family, her childhood friends and the country set she had grown up with, Helen had hated being banished to distant Moorehampstead. Nevertheless, Bert would not relent. Faldwell was too close to the war, it was 'not safe'. Helen would retort: 'As if anywhere's safe, these days!' But Bert was nothing if not a man who knew his own mind. In this he was unbending. Helen and the children had remained in Gloucestershire, sharing the cottage outside Cheltenham with his increasingly dotty Aunt Phoebe. A lesser man than Bert would have known that Helen would take her revenge.

From the start Adam was a frequent visitor to the cottage, staying there on his trips down to Cornwall to visit his sister, Henrietta, in Tavistock. He would pay his respects to the old lady, talk, flirt harmlessly with Helen. Occasionally, Bert would make a flying appearance and they would roll down to the village ale house. More usually Bert would be absent, Adam would exchange pleasantries with the old lady, swap gossip about mutual acquaintances and reminiscences of Faldwell with Helen.

And then Adam was posted to Marwood Lodge, less than an hour's drive from Moorehampstead. One evening, things had got out of hand. It had started as a harmless game, no more. Suddenly the flirting had stopped and he and Helen had ended up in each other's arms as if it was the most natural thing in the world.

'I never thought you'd come through a tour,' Helen had said to him once, tearfully. Later he realised she had been trying to make him understand how she could live the lie. 'I didn't think either of you would. Now you've come through it's as if you've been given back your life. For a while at least. Until you have to go back, again.'

Appearances had been maintained. Secrets kept. In the beginning they were outrageously lucky. Later they had learned to be careful, mindful of watching eyes. Adam was a part of the family, his presence taken for granted; young Jack Fulshawe's godfathers had been killed on the way back from Wilhelmshaven and he had stepped into their empty shoes. He always brought presents, took Helen for a spin in the Bentley, dug the garden in spring, in the autumn swept the leaves, chopped wood for the fire. He came and went without warning or comment or hindrance. The children would tease Rufus until even his placid temper frayed and he turned fractious, the family would gather round the fire, the children would chatter. Helen, who was six years her husband's junior, would sit in the shadows, reading a book, listening to the radio, darning socks. Adam would make great play of settling himself to sleep in an armchair, and would always depart before dawn.

Aunt Phoebe was none the wiser.

Neither was Bert, and now he was gone.

The last time Adam had passed through Gloucestershire Bert had actually been in residence, they had played cricket with Jack in the garden behind the cottage. Helen had served up a rabbit and vegetable stew, the children - worn out by the afternoon's play - had been packed off to bed early and he and Bert had propped up the bar of the nearby Fox and Hounds, talked shop into the night. They were familiar faces in the village and stayed behind after closing time drinking with the Publican, standing rounds for the Inn's regulars. They had stumbled home, arm in arm, blind drunk. The next morning Adam had awakened in a heap by the fire. Helen had pushed a cushion under his head and spread a thick, warm blanket over his unconscious body. Bert was already up and about, as fresh as a daisy and completely unaffected by the excesses of the night before. Adam on the other hand, had carried around a thick head for days afterwards. That was in June. The day before he took command at Waltham Grange.

He tried to picture Helen in widow's black, tears running down her fair cheeks but no matter how hard he tried to see her otherwise, all he saw was the paleness of her breasts, exquisite, small rounded mounds heaving beneath him in the moonlight, the soft stirring of her breath, her lips half-open, sighing as he moved deep inside her. It was as if she was with him even now. The scent of her hair was in his face, her laughter rang in his ears and he craved her, longed to have her and to hold her, to roll with her again in the big, warm bed in the darkness of the night. Or to bury himself in her amidst the spring daffodils, or behind a hedgerow, or in the long grass, or up against the bedroom door. The remembrance of first love turned sour, of crumbling dreams struck him to the quick. The pain was physical, stabbing. He had honestly believed that he had let go of Helen; learned to live without her.

"It's over!" He snarled to himself, gunning the motor viciously, wrenching the car around the next bend. "Over!"

Turning off the Lincoln Road and cutting across country the Bentley was slowed to a growling, unhappy crawl, stuck behind a convoy of big blue and grey fuel bowsers grinding along the narrow lanes.

It was nearly one o'clock by the time he reached Waltham Grange to discover that another big raid was in the offing.

"Maximum effort to Mannheim," declared Group Captain Henderson as Adam stuck his head around the door of his office. "8 Group are mounting a diversionary show over Darmstadt to draw off the fighters."

"Oh." Maximum Effort calls on consecutive nights were unusual because the logistical nightmare of a major raid normally took up to forty-eight hours to fully unravel.

"How many aircraft are we offering Group, sir?"

"Fourteen, presently. The maintenance chief thinks we might bump that up to sixteen or seventeen by the off."

"Good. Do we have any more news on last night's show?"

"Twenty-six heavies missing. Twelve Halifaxes, seven Lancs, five Stirlings and a couple of Wimpeys. Overall chop rate under four percent."

Adam paused for thought. 26 aircraft lost attacking a distant, dangerous target like Hanover represented a relatively low casualty rate. Significantly, the Lancaster Force - over 300 aircraft - had once again suffered disproportionately lower losses than the rest of the bomber force.

"I take it Group have told you I'm to go up to Ansham Wolds, sir."

"Yes. The AOC briefed me over the scrambler link. I'm sorry to hear about Bert Fulshawe. You two were very close, I know."

Merlins were firing into life in the distance as the crews began to prepare for the op. The first item on the agenda was to flight test their big black steeds. This usually involved a circuit or two of the airfield, sometimes a short cross-country flight if major repairs had been carried out. Then the crews would have a meal and begin the round of specialist briefings; for bomb-aimers, navigators, engineers, gunners, which culminated in the final crew briefing two to three hours before the scheduled off. The roar of Merlins diverted Adam's thoughts, trapped him in a spell of remembrance.

"If you'll excuse me, sir."

Outside in the corridor he straightened his back, stood tall and marched towards the Operations Room. It was time to take control for one last time; to imprint his will and his experience on the Squadron's contribution to the evening's work. Bert Fulshawe was dead; there was nothing he could do about it. There would be plenty of time later, after the off, to try and find the words for a letter to Helen.

And to attempt to come to terms with the past.

Chapter 7

Thursday 23rd September, 1943
RAF Waltham Grange, Lincolnshire

Over 600 heavies had attacked the twin city of Mannheim-Ludwigshafen three weeks ago. Photographic reconnaissance showed a broad swath of destruction across the southern part of Mannheim, and the near total devastation of the central and southern districts of Ludwigshafen. Consequently, tonight's aiming point lay in the damaged but largely intact northern suburbs of Mannheim.

"It's not good enough to bomb in the Mannheim area," Adam stressed to his crews, summing up. "Bomb loads falling in the southern half of the city are wasted loads. There's nothing left to burn. Bomb-aimers, there are no excuses for getting it wrong tonight." He pointed his billiard cue at the heart of the target. "Make sure you check your aiming point against the bend in the Rhine."

He coughed, moved across to the lectern. The angle of approach to the target and the aiming point had been carefully calculated. Any 'creep back' in the bombing would cause widespread, new damage on the western bank of the Rhine in the city's relatively unscathed northern districts.

"There's another big spoof tonight. Pathfinder Force Lancs and Mosquitoes will be carrying out an attack on Darmstadt. Lots of TIs and flares again, just like last night diversion over Oldenburg. This attack should be in full swing by the time the first TIs go down on Mannheim. Last night the Oldenburg spoof forced the fighter controllers to split their forces. With a bit of luck they will repeat the same mistake tonight."

Adam laid aside the billiard cue. Moving away from the lectern he went to the front of the low stage and surveyed the faces of his crews.

"Normally, I'd wind things up, now," he explained, projecting his words to the corners of the long, smoky hall without seeming to raise or strain his voice. "However, this afternoon I have an announcement to make." He let the muttering exhaust itself. The hush descended. "I'm leaving 388 Squadron to assume command of 647 Squadron at Ansham Wolds. I shall be leaving Waltham Grange by the end of the week."

Momentarily, the silence was absolute. There was surprise, even a little shock on the faces of the men in the front rows. Adam took a deep breath and got on with what he had to say, knowing if he hesitated he was going to fluff his lines. That would never do.

"Gentlemen, it's been an honour serving with you." He wanted to run off the stage. There were tears in his eyes. "There are many things one ought to say on these occasions," he carried on, voice cracking. "But all I really want to say for now is that I wish I was coming with you tonight!"

Somebody yelled from the body of the hall: "Three cheers for the Wingco! Hip! Hip!"

The response was deafening.

"Hurrah!"

As one the crews jumped up, chairs scraped deafeningly. "Hip! Hip!"

"Hurrah!"

Feet stamped, caps were waved aloft. "Hip! Hip!"

"Hurrah!"

The cheers resounded in the hall, threatening to lift the roof. Adam was taken aback to such an extent that when at last the noise abated he was, for a second or perhaps, two or three, stunned. Then the ham actor in him stepped forward, took a bow and rescued the situation. He spread his arms to quell the high spirits.

"And tomorrow night," he promised, hoarsely. "We're going to have a bloody good party!" Later, he toured the dispersals as the crews waited for the order to mount up. As always on these occasions Ben Hardiman accompanied him but tonight the big man hung back, reluctant to intrude.

"You're quiet tonight, old man?"

"Just thinking, that's all," Ben grunted, defensively.

Adam strode off towards L-London's hard stand. Rufus padded along at his heels in the dark. Ben fell into step. The ground crew had already rolled the battery cart into position under the port wing of the Lancaster. L-London's crew were sprogs on their second operation.

"Ready for the off, Larry?" Adam asked the pilot.

"Yes, sir," reported the ashen-faced Sergeant Pilot, who was visibly startled by the god-like sudden appearance of the Wingco.

"Not long to go, now."

"No, sir."

"You'll feel better once you're in the air," Adam assured him, exuding calm authority. He looked round the circle of faces. "You'll all feel better once you're off. I always do. This is the worst time. It doesn't matter how many ops you've got under your belt, believe me. I used to be sick before every off."

Ben said nothing, he did not need to. His job was to stand at his friend's shoulder, to nod sagely as the aura of the man and his legend worked its magical spell. L-London's crew were scarcely more than boys, seven frightened children in the thrall of their seemingly indestructible CO. Adam's words took the edge off their fear, made the ghastliness of what awaited them over Germany a little more bearable. On the squadrons little things mattered, little things made *all* the difference and no man understood this better than Adam Chantrey. That was his secret, the thing that set him apart. Ben stood in the shadows. Adam chatted with the sprogs until the appointed hour arrived and one by one the boys clambered up into the big black bomber.

"Isn't it about time you told me about Ansham Wolds?" Ben shouted as all across Waltham Grange Merlins bellowed into life.

"Cold, wet, windy and miles from anywhere, old man!"

"I'm coming up to Ansham whether you like it or not!"

Adam turned to face him. He opened his mouth to speak.

Ben got his shot in first: "The chaps feel the same way! We're all coming with you! And that's that!"

Adam shut his mouth. Even though it went without saying he wanted Ben and the rest of the crew with him at Ansham Wolds, he ought to put his foot down. He ought to tell the big man to go to Hell. L-London's port-outer Merlin fired, whined briefly, turned over half-a-dozen times and picked up. In seconds it ran true, responded to throttle control, idling at zero boost. The air was full of sound, shaking softly.

"Look!" He shouted, hardly able to hear himself think, let alone speak. "That's as may be. You're screened, Ben. You're all screened!"

The big man shrugged, unimpressed.

Adam realised it was useless trying to reason with the him. So he resorted to a bare-faced lie.

"Look, you've all been screened. By the AOC. Nothing to do with me! They won't let me take anybody with me! No poaching! It's out of my hands!"

Ben sniffed, met his friend's gaze.

"That's a lot of bull and you know it!"

Adam looked away, unhappily, like small child caught stealing sweets. He knew better than try to mislead his friend. Ben was different. Ben knew him too well.

"Sorry," he said, abandoning all pretence.

"Good try," Ben said, leaning close to avoid having to shout.

"I think you're all mad!" Adam cried out over the rising crescendo of L-London's engines. Around the field still more Merlins were starting up, filling the air with thunder.

"We'd have to be to fly with a lunatic like you, Skipper!"

There were more tears now in Adam's eyes. Fortunately, the darkness hid them from his navigator. He turned his head away, saw L-London's pilot slide back the cockpit panel, thrust his hand out and give his ground crew a thumbs up signal. The bomber lurched forward, trundled clumsily towards the perimeter road. Adam waved both arms at the moving Lancaster, saw the pilot's face turn to look his way.

"Good luck, Larry!" He yelled.

The boy pilot gave his CO an exaggerated thumbs up, withdrew his arm, slammed the cockpit window shut and concentrated on the less than straightforward task of controlling the taxiing heavy. After the recent rain the infield was a quagmire. A wheel off the tarmac meant a protracted recovery exercise, a blocked road and a poor showing by the Squadron. L-London's boy pilot rolled the big bomber out onto the perimeter like an old hand, playing the brakes deftly, gunning the outer Merlins to correct the drift. The boy had a feel for his work and a rare empathy with his aircraft. Some men flew a Lancaster as if it was simply the sum of its fifty-five thousand miscellaneous parts and components. A few men - the chosen few - flew as if a Lancaster was a living, breathing entity, an extension of their own body. Young Larry belonged to this latter category, he was a born Lancaster pilot.

Adam turned, misty-eyed, and looked his friend in the eye.

"If you want to join me at Ansham that's fine by me. But I can't ask any of you to come with me. It's up to you! It has to be your decision!"

"That's settled then!"

Chapter 8

Friday 24th September, 1943
The Rectory, Ansham Wolds, Lincolnshire

Eleanor opened the gate and shepherded Johnny and Emmy along the path to the Rectory. Retrieving the key from beneath the upturned flower pot in the porch, she unlocked the big oaken front door. It had been a mild, cloudy day and there was more than a hint of rain in the air. Hopefully, the rain would hold off, otherwise she and the children were going to get wet walking home through the woods. She stooped, replaced the key where she had found it.

"Simon! Adelaide!" She called, shutting the door at her back. "You two go through to the parlour," she suggested to the children.

The Reverend Simon Naismith-Parry, tall grey and thin, emerged from his study, his reading glasses perched precariously on the end of his nose. He smiled benignly at Emmy, patted Johnny's head, and looked up at the youngsters' mother.

"Adelaide's retired to her bed," he explained, softly. "Her hip is troubling her more than somewhat, I fear."

Eleanor took off her coat and hung it on the peg in the hallway.

"How are you today, Simon?" She asked, stepping up to the old man and planting a brief, pecking kiss on his cheek. "I hope you've stayed in. Remember what the doctor said about your chest yesterday."

The Rector took the gentle scolding in good heart.

"I've been a model patient."

"I'm glad to hear it."

The Rector and his wife had welcomed Eleanor with open arms when she arrived in the village. They had been her only friends in those early days and now she watched over them. Adelaide was very frail, increasingly troubled with arthritis. Her husband was plagued by his weak chest but steadfastly refused to take care of himself, insisting on carrying on as if he was still a young man, hale and hearty. The Rector and Adelaide's only son, a Stirling pilot, had died the same month Eleanor's husband, Harry, had been killed in the Western Desert. Eleanor, the children, the Rector and his wife had become a new family; and Eleanor was devoted to the elderly couple like a daughter.

"Shall I put the kettle on?"

"Capital idea, my dear."

The Rector focussed his attention on Johnny and Emmy. "It's rather wet in the garden, I don't think your mummy would appreciate you getting covered in mud playing outside."

"No she won't!" Eleanor laughed, from the kitchen.

"So? What's it to be, a story or would you like me to read to you?"

"A story," the boy declared.

"Read!" Emmy demanded.

The old man grimaced. "A story then I shall read something," he compromised.

Eleanor busied herself in the kitchen. Soon the kettle was steaming. Outside the sky was quiet. The bombers had been away the last two nights. Big raids on successive nights were rare so she assumed the skies would be quiet tonight. She washed up the dishes from lunch, piled them on the drainer. Flecks of rain ran down the window. Presently, she took the tea tray into the parlour. Emmy was perched on the Rector's knee, listening avidly as he read from *The Wind in the Willows*. Johnny was a little restless, fidgeting.

"There was another big raid on Mannheim last night," the old man remarked when Eleanor had poured the tea. She sat in the armchair opposite the Rector, gathered Johnny onto her lap, hugged him and ruffled his hair.

"Tomorrow," she promised her son, "we shall go for a ramble up at the Hall. Would you like to do that?" The children were fascinated by the tumbled down ruins of Ansham Hall which sprawled across the hillside above the Gatekeeper's Lodge. Eleanor forbade them to play there alone, so visits to the old Hall were treats not to be scorned. "We'll pick berries, too. Shall we have blackberry crumble tomorrow evening? That would be nice, wouldn't it?"

Johnny nodded, reluctantly allowed himself to be cuddled even though he was reaching that age when boys begin to rail against such things. In public, leastways.

"Blackberry crumble," murmured the Rector. "Is it that time of year again, already? Where does time go?"

"I wish I knew," Eleanor sighed. "So it was Mannheim again last night?"

"Apparently. The BBC says that thirty-two of our aircraft are missing."

"Oh."

The Rector sipped his tea. The fire in the hearth flickered and crackled, its warmth bathing his face and lighting the bright eyes of the children. "I really ought to look in on Adelaide," he announced.

"Stay there, Simon," Eleanor rebuked him with a smile. "I'll go."

The old man had learned not to argue with her.

Eleanor hugged her son, ticked him in the

ribs and when he laughed put her face close to his, her smiling eyes gazing happily into his. The boy put his arms around her neck and she lifted him up, twirled about in a half circle.

"See. Things aren't so bad, darling?"

Johnny was shy for a moment. Then he shook his head.

"No, mummy."

Chapter 9

Friday 24th September, 1943
RAF Waltham Grange, Lincolnshire

The party was in full swing but Adam wanted time alone. There were loose ends to be tied up and last rites to be performed before he surrendered the Squadron. From the Mess the strains of voices lustily, raucously raised in song drifted into his office.

"Things seem to be warming up, sir," the Adjutant observed, knocking at the open door.

Adam looked up from the report he was reading. "Sorry, what was that?" As if on cue the sound of distant voices leaked into the room, carried on the breeze. He had shut Rufus away. For some reason the chaps took a perverse delight in getting his faithful hound tipsy.

"There'll be a few sore heads in the morning, sir."

"Oh. Yes, no doubt." Adam was immersed in paperwork, determined to bequeath his successor an empty in tray.

"I can take care of most of this, you know," the Adjutant reminded him, waving sternly at the heaps of files. "Everything's in good order. You've seen to that, sir. I think the chaps really would appreciate your presence, sir."

Adam frowned. The older man stood before him unflinching, clasping a thin Manila folder.

"Later. Are those the letters?"

"Yes, sir."

Once upon a time Adam had written personally to the next of kin of his missing aircrew. Therein lay ruin. At Waltham Grange the Adjutant had prevailed upon him to leave matters in his hands. Last night the Main Force had ploughed a great furrow of new destruction across the northern districts of Mannheim-Ludwigshafen but one of his Lancasters was among the 32 heavies that had failed to return from Germany: L-London. So tonight there were another seven letters to sign. The Adjutant moved around the desk and laid the sheaf of letters on Adam's blotter. "Normal format, sir."

"Thank you."

The Adjutant made a discreet exit. The Wingco was nothing if not a creature of habit. Before he signed the letters he would read each one slowly, painstakingly, sometimes many times over. Adam did not notice the other man leave. His gaze had fallen on the first letter.

L-London's crew was the eighteenth crew posted 'missing' in the three months he had commanded 388 Squadron. During that time the squadron had participated in 26 major attacks on targets in Germany, and 6 operations - mostly milk runs - against targets in Italy. In baldly statistical terms 18 missing Lancasters and the 126 men in them represented a casualty rate of about four percent of all sorties despatched on ops.

More or less par for the course.

The mark of a good squadron was its ability to ride out heavy losses over the short term while retaining its fighting spirit - its capacity to 'press on' - over the longer haul. Lately, 388 Squadron had more than proved its capacity to press on. Back in June and early July the Squadron had had a middlingly bad trot; 13 heavies lost in ten operations, including 4 in an attack on Gelsenkirchen. Thereafter, Waltham Grange's luck had changed for the better: a bloodless trip to Essen, a milk run to Turin and the Squadron had turned the corner, not losing a single aircraft to enemy action throughout the whole of August. Eventually, of course, the odds - what staff officers like to call the 'law of averages' and what aircrew called 'sod's law' - had caught up with the Squadron. September had taken a new toll on his crews: 2 aircraft failing to return from Berlin, others going missing over Munich, and now Mannheim-Ludwigshafen, raising the month's butcher's bill to 5 crews.

The men lost in June and July had been

strangers. Not so the missing men in September. Every man was known to him, each man embraced by the brotherhood of the Squadron.

Adam forced himself to read the first letter.

```
Reference:-   No.   388   Squadron,
AC/9/43
RAF Station,
Waltham Grange, Lincs.


24th. September, 1943


My Dear Mrs Wilkinson,
   It is with deep regret that I
write to confirm my telegram
advising you that your son,
Sergeant L.G. Wilkinson, is
missing as a result of operations
on the night of 23/24th
September, 1943.
   Your son was the pilot of an
aircraft detailed to carry out an
attack on Mannheim. Contact was
lost with this aircraft after it
took off, and nothing further has
been heard from it.
   It is possible that the crew
were able to abandon the aircraft
and land safely in enemy
territory, in which event news
```

will reach you direct from the International Red Cross Committee within the next six weeks.

Although, Larry had only been on the squadron a short time, he had made a great impression with us all. He was a popular aircraft captain and a very able pilot, and I am sure, would have done everything possible to ensure the safety of his crew.

Please accept my sincere sympathy during this anxious period of waiting.

I have arranged for your son's personal effects to be taken care of by the Committee of Adjustment Officer at this Station, and these will be forwarded to you through normal channels in due course.

If there is any way in which I can help you, please let me know.

Yours Sincerely,

Wing-Commander,

<u>Commanding, 388 Squadron, RAF</u>

It was the first of seven letters.

The use of the word 'missing' was, of course, a misnomer. For a pilot, missing over enemy territory actually meant 'missing presumed dead'. A pilot might be able to hold his aircraft straight and level after it was hit; long enough perhaps for some or all of his crew to get out but the moment he released the controls the aircraft would fall out of the sky, centrifugal force would pin him to his seat or smash him senseless. Either way he would be trapped, doomed barring some extraordinary freak circumstance.

In Adam Chantrey's lexicon 'missing' invariably meant 'dead'.

Tonight his crews were celebrating their survival, making merry in the time they had left to them. If there was a time to mourn the fallen it was not now; too many forms of death stalked the bomber stream and only a fool dwelled overlong on the unknown and the unknowable. When a Squadron paused to mourn its fallen it was almost the beginning of the end.

You had to look towards tomorrow.

Whatever happened, you had to believe that there was a tomorrow.

Adam realised it was time he joined his crews.

He signed the letter to Mrs. Wilkinson. Afterwards, he signed the letters to Mrs. Owen, Mr. Goodall, Mrs. Sidney, Mr. Berry, Miss Calder-Brown, and Mr. McLeod; letters bound for two more widowed mothers, three fathers, and a sister. None of the missing aircrew had been married. The oldest among them was twenty-two, the youngest, nineteen. Carefully, almost reverentially, he collected the letters and replaced them in the Manila folder.

On his way to the Mess he stopped off at the darkened Squadron Office and placed the folder in the Adjutant's in tray.

Then he went back to the party.

Chapter 10

Saturday 25th September, 1943
No. 1 Group Headquarters, Bawtry Hall, South Yorkshire

Since the outbreak of war a motley overspill of Nissen huts and prefabricated sheds had colonized the rolling grounds of Bawtry Hall, an ivy-clad, once grand house. Out of sight, buried deep beneath the neglected lawns and tennis courts where county gentry had once whiled away inter-war summer afternoons, there was a warren of bomb shelters and bunkers.

Regardless of events over Germany the Group's Headquarters staff, like topsy, had grown and grown. Now, after four long years of war the Group was about to begin yet another expansion. New squadrons were to be raised, new stations opened and wherever practical, the establishments of existing formations increased from two to three flights. Within a year the Group's front line strength of around two hundred operational Lancasters was set to nearly double, to between three and four hundred heavies. To accommodate the anticipated influx of pen pushers a fresh wave of building activity was under way. Beyond the immediate environs of the Hall, Bawtry

Park resembled a construction site.

Adam parked the Bentley behind the Hall. Heavy overnight rain had muddied the paths and turned the whole area into a bog. Duck boards stretched from hut to hut, and wherever tarmac or paving stones gave way to turf or earth the morass was inches deep. Steady rain descended as he got out of the car. Motioning Rufus to follow him, he headed purposefully off into the swamp. His first port of call was the huge plywood shed housing the office of the Wing-Commander (Personnel). Great-coated figures splashed past him, hurrying to get out of the wet. Adam, swathed in his sheepskin flying jacket was oblivious to the rain. Mostly, on account of the fact he was still extremely hung over from the previous night's excesses.

Inside, the Wing-Commander (P) - with whom Adam had had more than one bad-tempered verbal joust in recent weeks - was nowhere to be found. Instead, he was referred to a grey-haired, portly squadron leader who hurriedly, and very apologetically explained that his chief was in hospital in Doncaster, suffering from a suspected perforated duodenal ulcer.

"He's been under a lot of strain," remarked the older man, sweeping a hand through his thinning hair.

"I'm sorry to hear it," Adam said, his tone pointedly lacking in compassion. "You chaps must be under a lot of pressure, these days."

The other man smiled an uneasy smile. Although he was a newcomer to Bawtry Hall, the Wing-Commander (P) had warned him about Adam Chantrey. Warned him in no uncertain terms. The boy was a firebrand, a staff officer's worst nightmare.

"Yes, sir," he agreed, trying to ignore the fact that his visitor's over-sized Alsatian was investigating his wastepaper basket and was on the verge of overturning it. "I have your orders, sir. I'm afraid I must ask you to sign for them. Just a formality. Standing Orders, sir. I'm sure you understand."

Adam was watching Rufus out of the corner of his eye, wondering idly what the dog had found in the bin. The basket tipped over, its contents spilled across the floor. He looked up, dull-eyed.

"Understand?"

The squadron leader swallowed, nervously.

"Standing orders, sir."

"Rufus," Adam muttered sidelong at the dog. Obediently, Rufus lifted his snout from the rubbish, and came to heel by his master's side. "Good boy."

He signed for his orders without further ado.

"The Ops Officer asked if you'd care to drop in on him, sir. Before you left for Ansham Wolds."

"Oh?" The main reason for Adam's visit to Bawtry Hall was to catch up with key members of the Operations Staff and have first sight of any new technical papers in their possession. This possibility clearly had not occurred to the pen-pushers in the 'Personnel Shed'.

"If it was convenient, sir."

"Thank you."

Outside the rain had eased a little. Adam tore open the envelope, cast a cursory eye over the contents before the letter started to disintegrate in the rain. There were no surprises, no caveats, no traps. The wording was succinct. He, being 'AWH Chantrey, DSO, DFC', etcetera ad nauseam, 'Wing-Commander, RAF, was required to report to the Air Officer Commanding RAF Ansham Wolds, Lincolnshire, not later than 24:00 hours 25th September, 1943, thereupon to assume command of No. 647 (Bomber) Squadron...' And so on.

The Operations Staff was located within the walls of Bawtry Hall; inside the mansion Rufus attracted significantly more attention than his master. Wing-Commanders might lead the Group's squadrons into battle but in these rarefied, cloistered surroundings, they were two a penny. Rufus's paws left a wet, muddy trail down the polished corridor floors as Adam led him deep into the bowels of the building. He headed straight for the office of the Operations Officer.

In the ante room a booming voice rang out.

"I say! That man! You can't bring that bloody animal in here!"

Adam spun around.

"Hello, Pat," he grinned.

The Group Operations Officer beamed broadly at him from the other side of the room. Rufus picked up his ears and bounded towards him. The dog jumped up to enthusiastically renew an old friendship, almost bowling over the stout figure of Wing-Commander Patrick Farlane. This despite the fact the latter had taken the precaution of bracing himself against the side of a desk. Farlane fought off the dog, laughing. He limped over to Adam.

"Come through to my den," he insisted, grabbing the younger man's arm, clapping him enthusiastically on the back.

He shut the door at his back and they were alone. Adam directed Rufus to lie down and reluctantly, the dog did as he was bade.

"I got your message that you wanted a word, Pat?"

"Several, actually," Farlane replied,

cheerfully twirling one wing of his magnificent handlebar moustache.

Adam sensed his old friend's joviality was a trifle forced. He and Pat were members of an increasingly select club in Bomber Command; survivors of the December 1939 Wilhelmshaven raid. After Wilhelmshaven it had fallen to Pat to rebuild the Squadron, only for his own ops career to be prematurely curtailed by a training accident the following spring; he had lost a leg and very nearly his life inadvertently parking his Wellington in Faldwell Fen. Somehow, Pat had persuaded the powers that be to let him return to active service, even to fly again. Albeit not on ops. At least, not officially. Unofficially, Pat had more than once hitched a lift to Germany on one or other of Adam's Lancasters in the last year. A little over a month ago Adam had had the pleasure of personally escorting him on a midnight tour of the Unter den Linden from a height of twenty-one thousand feet.

"I'm all ears."

"What's this damned fool story about you taking over at Ansham?"

Adam chuckled. Pat Farlane never changed. No beating about the bush.

"If it wasn't me it would be somebody else, old man."

"I take it you've heard about Bert?"

Adam nodded.

"From the Station Master, no doubt?"

"Yes. Group Captain Alexander seems a decent sort."

Pat scowled at the younger man.

"Alex? Oh, yes. Absolute salt of the earth," he confirmed, dropping behind his desk.

Adam dug out his cigarettes. They lit up. Easing himself into the chair opposite Pat he summoned the courage to meet his friend's eye.

"Nobody's twisting my arm, you know."

Pat sighed, knowing that nobody would have had to twist his arm. That was not the way things worked and they both knew it. Adam Chantrey was an ops man pure and simple. He had known nothing else, had no other adult life. The arrogant, reckless boy he had known at Faldwell in the first winter of the war had grown to manhood on the squadrons of the Main Force. He had flown low across France by day to bomb the Schneider armament works at Le Creusot. He had flown over the Alps by moonlight to bomb the cities of northern Italy. Mostly, he had flown the long cold roads to the German heartland. Well over sixty times, by Pat's count. And as if this was not enough for one man, between bomber tours Adam had turned poacher, hunted Dorniers, Heinkels and Junkers in the night skies over Britain; shooting down at least four enemy aircraft. One more kill and they would have classified him as an 'ace'. He would have hated that; they would have never allowed a night fighter ace back on bomber ops.

"No," Pat murmured. "Of course not. About Bert. I dashed off a letter to Helen, as soon as I found out what happened. Told her a pack of lies about Bert pressing on, and all that guff. No need for her to know what really happened, what? Mum's the word, what?"

Adam stared at his feet.

"Absolutely."

"Jolly good." Farlane had worked out what was going on between Helen Fulshawe and Adam fairly early in the game and decided that he was not going to take sides. There was a war going on, peace time standards did not apply and he had no intention of re-opening old wounds, now. Bert Fulshawe was dead. They had lost another friend, perhaps their dearest and longest surviving friend in the whole world. The past was the past and they were both, in their own way, as equally in Bert Fulshawe's debt. His memory was going to be honoured. And that was that! "Have you written to Helen, yet?"

"Er, no. Not had time."

"As I say, mum's the word."

"Whatever you say."

"A crash," Pat said, reaching into the bottom drawer of his desk and pulling out a pair of dusty cups. He blew off the cobwebs, brushed each on his sleeve. Then, producing a silver hip flask, he poured generous measures of a clear, amber fluid into each glass. "Bert always wanted to go out in a blaze of glory, what!"

"I'll make up something plausible," Adam agreed, distractedly.

"Good man."

"What are we drinking to?"

"Absent friends!"

Adam took the glass he was offered, raised it high.

"Bert Fulshawe." The whisky burned his throat.

"Going up to Ansham Wolds is a damned fool thing to do!"

"If you were me, what would you do, Pat?"

The older man twirled one end of his moustache. That was a damnably unfair question. Below the belt. In his friend's place he would have leapt at the chance, grabbed it with both hands without a second thought.

"I'd probably go up the Ansham Wolds," he confessed, grudgingly. "But it would still be a damned fool thing to do!"

The sun made a series of fleeting appearances as Adam drove across the fertile, rolling farmlands east of Gainsborough. Although he had never visited Ansham Wolds, he was intimately acquainted with the lie of the land between him and his destination. He headed west along the road to Market Rasen. Beyond Hemswell he turned left at Caenby Corner onto the A15, headed north along the arrow straight path of the road the Romans had known as Ermine Street. At Kirton-in-Lindsey the modern road branched north-east, through Hibaldstow and on to Brigg. Hereabouts the land undulated; aerodromes were scarcer than on the plains around Lincoln. In the east the long, misty grey chalk escarpment of the Lincolnshire Wolds filled the horizon. Atop the high wolds between three and four hundred feet above sea level lay a string of 1 Group stations: Ludford Magna, Binbrook, Kirmington, Elsham Wolds and Ansham Wolds.

The village of Thurlby-le-Wold sheltered in the valley of the Ansham Brook. To the north and south the land rose steeply. A train was pulling into the station as Adam drove down into the Vale of Thurlby. The trees were still in full leaf, and crops unharvested in some of the higher fields. Wisps of smoke curled above red-brick cottages. He slowed the Bentley to a crawl as a bus disgorged a cargo of men and women in RAF blue outside the railway station.

No ops today.

Further on, he came to a crossroads. Ahead the road narrowed, swept out of sight into the trees. He swung the Bentley over an ancient stone bridge, engaged a low gear and followed the road up the south-facing slope of the valley. The trees became sparser and the cultivated fields gave way to enclosures where sheep grazed. On his right he read a faded signpost for *Grafton Hall*, another for *Ansham Wolds*. He drove straight on. The land above the valley was turning autumnal, hues of brown and dull gold mingling with faded Lincoln green.

At the gates of RAF Ansham Wolds the guard snapped smartly to attention, and waved the Bentley through with a minimum of ceremony. In the middle distance the aerodrome buildings jutted bleakly out of the landscape; massive hangars loomed in the haze, distantly a tall water tower, and nearby the glass-fronted watchtower. Row upon row of Nissen-hutted barracks, workshops, offices and store rooms marched across the rim of the high wold, and in the far distance he could just discern the dark, menacing forms of several of the Squadron's Lancasters standing sentinel at their dispersals. Small things caught his eye as he looked for the sign for the squadron office: bicycles propped up against a wall, two WAAFs walking by in conversation not giving the car a second glance, an erk scurrying towards the hangars with a sheaf of papers under his arm, and a group of civilian workers smoking, drinking tea around a churning cement mixer.

He strolled into the squadron office with Rufus at his heels.

"Wing-Commander Chantrey, sir?" Beamed a balding, middle-aged flight-lieutenant wearing horn-rimmed spectacles who saluted like a civilian. "Welcome to Ansham Wolds, sir. I'm Tom Villiers. For my pains, the Adjutant, sir."

Adam viewed him hard-eyed for a moment. Then he relaxed a little.

"How do you do, Tom." He looked about him. A WAAF typist stood nervily to attention in the presence of the new Squadron Commander. A second WAAF, petite and blond peered at him curiously, fearlessly from behind the Adjutant's shoulder.

"The Group Captain is waiting for you in his office, sir."

Chapter 11

Saturday 25th September, 1943
RAF Ansham Wolds, Lincolnshire

Group Captain Alexander preceded his new Wing-Commander into the crowded Briefing Hall rather in the manner of Christ come to cleanse the Temple. Adam, strode stern-faced in his wake up the long, narrow central aisle and was immediately aware of the sudden, unnatural hush. He stared at the Station Master's broad back as they marched towards the stage at the far end of the hall, looking neither to the left nor the right, grim-faced, very much Daniel walking into the lions' den.

Getting off on the right foot was everything.

Group Captain Alexander swept onto the stage and swung around to face the crews. Adam was struck by the change in the older man. Two days ago at Bawtry Hall he had seemed sick and tired, resigned. Today, he was a new man, rejuvenated, vital.

And...angry.

Adam listened to Alexander's preamble with half-an-ear as his gaze roved across the nearest faces. While the Group Captain's voice boomed in the background like distant artillery fire he was gauging the mood in the hall. Resentment was in plentiful supply. He could feel it in the air: it charged the atmosphere, became thicker with every word the Station Master uttered. Probably a good sign. The resentment of proud men living in the shadow of failure was something he understood. Something he could respect. Something he could work with and hopefully, turn to his advantage.

Finally, the Station Commander surrendered the floor.

Adam was in no hurry.

Advancing slowly to the front of the stage, he coughed to clear his throat. He was a stranger to most of the men in the hall and this afternoon he was glad of the fact. In this company of strangers his composure would seem perfect. He placed his hands squarely on his hips. He knew exactly what he wanted to say, how he was going to say it and how it was likely to go down with the crews. It was best not to be surprised on these occasions. That was one of the many lessons he had learned from Bert Fulshawe. However, even though his old friend was much in his thoughts; Bert had no part in the future for him, or for these crews. Bert was gone. Today there would be no mention of his name, or of his death because this and *every* day to come, was a day for the living.

"Take a good look at me, gentlemen!" His

voice carried down the hall, an icy, brutal thing. Stony, hostile silence welcomed him to Ansham Wolds. "Some of you think that I've been sent here to sort you out!" He paused for effect. "Perhaps, I have been sent here to sort you out. Bang some heads together. Perhaps. You've been through a bad patch. You've got yourselves a bit of a bad name. It happens! Sometimes it happens to the best of us! Sometimes there's nothing you can do about it! Sometimes it's not your fault! You do all the right things and things still go wrong!" Abruptly, he walked to the left edge of the stage. "Frankly, I don't give a damn what people say about Ansham Wolds. I don't give a damn about what's gone on here in the past. The past is the past. What's gone is gone! Over and done with! Finished!"

Adam scanned the faces in the crowd, searching for signs that some of the crews - particularly the younger ones - had taken his words to heart.

"What I want to say to you is that things will change, gentlemen!" In saying it he allowed the pitch of his voice to fall. "You've probably heard that before." Several men in the front row nodded. "That's as may be. But believe me: things will change!"

He strode back to the centre of the stage.

"Mindful that good drinking time is going

wasting, I shall keep this short and to the point, gentlemen. Whether you like it or not, you are stuck with *me*. So, in the interests of, shall we say, mutual understanding, there are several matters upon which I intend to make my views absolutely clear from the outset!"

This raised a number of jaundiced eyebrows and the first audible groans from the body of the hall.

"First," Adam grated. "I cannot and I will not abide fringe-merchants!" This was spat out like a curse. "From now on the photo-flash delay mechanism in all 647 Squadron aircraft will be triggered by the release of the largest high explosive bomb carried on your Lancs. From now on anybody who comes back from an op without an aiming point print will have a great deal of explaining to do!"

The majority of the crews greeted this news with a surly silence. Not so several of the Squadron's senior officers, seated behind him on the stage. There was a sharp intake of breath by more than one man. Adam ignored it. He had touched a raw nerve, drawn blood.

Good!

"Second," he went on. "In my book there are two sorts of early returners. Those who get court-martialled and those whose aircraft are demonstrably defective. I repeat. I won't have fringe-merchants on my Squadron. A crew that brings home a sound aircraft without first pressing home its attack is an abomination. An abomination! If there is any man in this hall who hasn't got his heart in it, then he can report to me directly we finished here. This afternoon! There is no place for him here!"

While his audience digested this he struck again, the iron now glowing red hot in his hands.

"Third. I do not and never have, subscribed to the leadership by committee school of command. I do not regard the Royal Air Force as the finest flying club in the world, and I do not regard any part of what we do here as a game. I am in charge now, gentlemen, be assured that I am in deadly earnest when I tell you that from now on you will do things my way! And only my way!"

Many of the men in the hall would live a lot longer if they did things his way. The trick was to make them believe it.

"Fourth. This Squadron will be flying operations again at squadron strength by the end of the next moon period." The announcement caused a stir in the hall. "This will mean a great deal of hard work. A great deal of hard work for us all! Your Flight Commanders will be authorised to issue twelve hour off-station passes. Otherwise, all leave is cancelled until such time as 647 Squadron is fully restored to the order of battle!"

The young faces in the front row were pale and pinched from living in the cold twilight and the darkness of the night, ashen from the bite of the frost at twenty thousand feet over Germany.

So young...

"Lastly. You will at all times treat my dog like a member of the family." He allowed himself a half-smile, but the edict was delivered with every bit as much vehemence as those which had gone before it. "An old and much respected member of the family! That will be all, gentlemen!"

Dismissing the crews he went to work.

His new office was Spartan. Unlike his previous station Ansham Wolds was a wartime creation. Whereas, Waltham Grange had been established in the twenties, developed painstakingly in the thirties and methodically expanded to cope with the demands of the new generation of heavies, Ansham Wolds was a starker, harsher place by far. A crueller place. There were few red brick buildings, practically everything was prefabricated and had been thrown up at breakneck speed.

His room – Bert Fulshawe's old room - in the Mess stank of disinfectant and fresh paint. The Adjutant had suggested a different billet, observed that there were several spare. There were always spare billets on the Squadrons.

"Recent casualties," Tom Villiers had explained, unnecessarily.

"No," Adam had decided, looking around. "This will do."

"We found Wing-Commander Fulshawe beside his writing table, sir. It was by the window. The table, that is."

"Yes." The disinfectant and the paint had brutally exorcised the last vestiges of Bert Fulshawe's existence from his quarters.

"I gather you knew Wing-Commander Fulshawe, sir?"

Adam had nodded. "Bert was at Stowe with my brother."

"Oh, I see."

"Later on he was my Flight Commander at Faldwell. We had some rare old spills together."

"I can imagine."

"Would you leave alone me a few minutes please, Tom?"

"Of course, sir."

Adam had sat on the bed, smoked a cigarette, tried to pull himself together. He had expected to feel Bert's presence about him, hoped to make his peace with his old friend's ghost but now in the cold light of day he realised how ridiculous such thoughts were. The stench of the disinfectant stung his nostrils. He was wasting time. *"Stop feeling sorry for yourself!"* There was too much to be done, no time to dwell on his mistakes.

Snatching a hurried meal of spam and potatoes, he had gone to his new office, called for his in tray and set about getting intimately acquainted with Ansham Wolds. The Adjutant, Tom Villiers, a country solicitor before the war, hovered by his shoulder, helpfulness personified and a font of concise local knowledge.

Rufus's big battered basket had been placed on the floor beside his master's desk. Adam had mentioned to Villiers, in passing, that Rufus was partial to stout, and a mug had miraculously appeared on the floor by his basket. The dog had lapped at its contents loudly, enthusiastically, and shortly thereafter retired for a contented nap.

Adam summoned his Flight Commanders to a late afternoon conference. They had arrived together a few minutes before the appointed hour.

"Barney Knight, sir. I'm B Flight," declared the first to speak in a voice that was pure Oxbridge. The senior Flight Commander's eyes were blue and steady and he spoke with the confidence of a man who was playing on his home ground.

The other man was a little older, Adam's

own age. He was less sure of himself. "McDonald, sir. Ewan McDonald. The chaps call me Mac. I'm in charge of A Flight. Acting, anyway. Since last month, sir." Adam recognised the soft, border accent, recognised also the fact that McDonald had plainly not enjoyed a proper night's sleep in weeks. If Knight wore his worries on his sleeve, the Scot carried them squarely on his back.

Hands were shaken.

"Sit down, gentlemen."

Adam settled in his chair, studied the pair over the heaped paperwork on his desk. He had skimmed through both men's files. Squadron Leader Barney Knight was commander of B Flight because he was born to it; Flight-Lieutenant Ewan McDonald commanded A Flight because he had outlived all of his contemporaries. In Bomber Command survival was a gift from the gods; not a thing to be taken lightly, and in many ways a recommendation second to none.

"Let's not mess about," Adam began, brusquely. Knight and McDonald wanted to be reassured that, despite appearances, the new Wingco was a good egg. He was going to have to risk disappointing them. "How many airworthy Lancs with crews do we have?"

"Thirteen or fourteen, sir," Knight replied. "I think."

"You think?"

"Fourteen, sir."

"What about ready for ops?" Adam viewed Knight with a decidedly jaundiced eye. The younger man shifted uneasily in his chair. "Fourteen? Ready for ops? I was given to understand we had a problem here? Perhaps, the AOC got hold of the wrong end of the stick?"

It was at this juncture McDonald entered the fray. "If we were asked for fourteen or fifteen aircraft for tonight we would find them, sir. Aircraft and crew availability isn't the problem." It was said with a dogged disregard for the likely wrath of his new CO.

Adam liked that. He liked it a lot because it told him straight away that at least one of his Flight Commanders was a man with whom he could do business. He wasted no time testing this first impression.

"And what exactly is the problem, Mac?"

"We have too many new crews. And more Lancs than we have experienced crews to fly them; or for that matter enough experienced erks to keep them flying, sir."

Adam nodded, lit up a cigarette.

"Right now it doesn't matter how many Lancs we've got," he said it quietly, dispassionately. "Right now the AOC thinks 647 Squadron is a shambles."

Barney Knight protested instantly: "I think that's a bit unfair, sir!"

Adam waved away Knight's protest.

"Since the end of July 647 Squadron has been top of the early-returners league, dropped a lower percentage of bombs on target than any other full-strength formation, and suffered the highest chop rate in the Group. I'd say the Squadron's a shambles, wouldn't you? No? Never mind. I'm not here to rake over the coals. For what it's worth I'm not much of a chap for inquests. And even if I was, we haven't got time for any of that guff. Three weeks from now I'm going to report to the AOC that 647 Squadron is fit to resume operations at squadron strength. No ifs, no buts, gentlemen. *This* Squadron will be fit for operations in three weeks time!"

Rufus chose this moment to rise from his basket. He shook himself, stretched and padded around the corner of the desk to stare up at his master. "Walkies, gentlemen," Adam declared, taking the hint.

Donning his sheepskin flying jacket he set off across the field towards the dispersals in the near distance. His bemused Flight Commanders trooped after him, curious and a little uncertain about what was going to happen next. Rufus trotted ahead of the trio, stopping frequently to sniff the air and to investigate the unfamiliar surroundings.

Adam rubbed his hands together.

"I want up to date reports on the training requirements of your crews on my desk by twelve hundred hours tomorrow. I need to know what we can expect of our crews and your recommendations as to how we go about improving their operational readiness. Then I want you to plan a programme of high and low-level navigation exercises across country. And over water, of course. From now on all exercises are to be flown at simulated operational take-off weights. Base your plans on the premise that I want every crew in the air for at least four hours a day. Whether or not this is feasible given the kind of weather we can reasonably expect at this time of year remains to be seen, but we'll worry about that later."

Knight cleared his throat.

"Our monthly non-ops fuel allocation won't go that far, sir."

"Then we'll have to get it increased, Barney! You get the crews in the air, I'll sort out the fuel!" Adam halted, shoved his hands into his pockets. Fuel was the least of his problems. Nobody at Group was actually going to court-martial him for exceeding the Squadron's 100-octane allocation. He breathed deep, exhaled the frigid autumnal air. Dusk was settling over the high wold and around them the bleak expanse of the aerodrome stretched away into the mist. Faraway, Lancasters stood blurred and indistinct, not a single Merlin turned as across Lincolnshire the Main Force rested for another night. "God, I'd forgotten how beautiful it is up here!"

Knight frowned. McDonald allowed himself a smile. The lonely windswept grandeur of the station often reminded him of his native Borders.

"Training, gentlemen," Adam went on. "Training is what distinguishes an army from a rabble. Or in our case it is what distinguishes live crews from dead crews. While we may not have any control over tactics, we have a great deal of control over the operational preparedness of our crews. So, our first step towards putting the Squadron to rights will be to ensure that no man flies ops unless one of us has personally satisfied himself that man is ready to fly ops. Nobody. No exceptions. From now on nobody goes swanning off on ops unless we've done everything possible to give that man a fighting chance."

"How would define a fighting chance, sir?" This from Knight who was unable to conceal his scepticism.

"Good question," Adam replied. "I don't think we can settle on any hard and fast rules.

It's a matter of judgement. Old lag's common sense, if you like. We three are the oldest lags at Ansham Wolds so if we don't know whether a chap's ready to fly ops then who does?"

McDonald nodded. The mist was rising off the ground. It was cold, very cold for a late September day and he wondered if this was an omen for the coming winter.

"Which leads me on to the second step in 647 Squadron's recovery," Adam said, shuffling into an ambling walk. "Conservation of resources. Specifically, conservation of the only resource to which I personally attach any importance. Our crews. At the risk of stating the patently bloody obvious, gentlemen, the Squadron's problems stem from one root cause. Not enough sprog crews are surviving long enough. Long enough, that is, to gain the experience needed to shepherd the *next* batch of sprog crews through their first few ops. Consequently, the Squadron's got a handful of experienced crews, and a mass of sprogs. There's no balance. The result is a vicious circle in which no sprog crew survives its first five ops. It's nobody's fault and for the record, I don't attribute any blame to either of you, but we *must* break the vicious circle. We must find ways of protecting our experienced crews."

In the Briefing Hall earlier that afternoon McDonald had feared Ansham Wolds had exchanged one madman for another. He now realised his fears had been groundless. Chantrey's analysis of what had gone wrong and what had to be done to repair the damage was nothing if not pragmatic. The Scot held his peace. This, he recognized, was a time to listen and to learn. Knight, on the other hand was having great difficulty tuning into the new Wingco's wavelength.

"That's all very well, sir," he objected, "but what does it mean in practice?"

"First off," Adam returned, evenly. "It means that you two are going to be flying a lot less ops in future. I've checked the Operations Record Book and you've been flying far too many ops. Particularly you, Barney. I can understand why and personally, I applaud your motives. Things have been going badly for the Squadron and you've been trying to lead from the front. Very commendable. However, there is a time and a place for heroics, and this, gentlemen, is not it!"

It was said with a quiet, implacable finality that left no room for debate. He looked to Barney, then Mac for confirmation that his edict had been taken onboard.

"I'm damned if I'm going to have you chaps flying yourselves into the ground. Until further notice I am restricting you to flying no more than two ops a month. I'll leave you to decide which ops you fly but under no circumstances will you both fly on the same op. Is that clear?"

"Crystal Clear," Knight grimaced.

"You both have regular crews, I take it?"

"Yes, sir," the Scot confirmed.

"Right, the same rules apply to them."

"Can we take it that these rules will also apply to you, too, sir?" Barney inquired, a tremor in his voice indicating that belatedly, he recognised he was taking his life in his hands. Mac braced himself for the explosion that never came. To his astonishment the new CO turned and grinned broadly.

"RHIP, Barney," he chuckled. "Rank hath its privileges!"

Even Knight was forced to smile.

"Where was I?" Adam demanded, rhetorically. "Conservation of resources. Aircraft don't matter. We can break as many of them as we like. The factories will always send us replacements. What we can't replace are experienced crews. Our problem is how to make sure our sprogs live long enough to gain experience, and once those sprogs have gained experience on ops, how we keep them alive for as long as possible thereafter. The only way you pick up operational experience is by flying ops. Unfortunately, the Operational Training Units aren't sending us chaps who are in any way qualified to fly ops. There's no point wasting time crying over spilt milk, the OTU situation is not going to change overnight. It's up to us to complete the operational training of our own crews. We can only do that by utilising our old lags, so basically, we can't let our old lags fly every op. By my reckoning, leaving out your own crews, we have one crew with sixteen ops under its belt, and five others who've completed at least a dozen ops. I want three of these crews to be withdrawn from ops until further notice so that we can form, immediately, a training flight within the Squadron. Initially, this flight will come directly under your command, Mac. This flight will act as an induction, conversion and operational training unit for all new crews."

Their feet rang out on tarmac. They had reached the edge of the main runway.

"Any questions, gentlemen?"

"Well, sir," Knight spoke up, oddly hesitant. "There was one thing, actually."

"Spit it out, Barney."

"This business about lashing up the photo-flash release to our cookies? Well, blow me, I don't know..."

"Not cricket?"

"Quite, sir. Not cricket. It doesn't seem right not giving our chaps the benefit of the doubt. Dash it all, sir! What happens if the camera's on the blink, or something?"

Although Mac could not see the Wingco's face in the gathering darkness, he visualised the bleakness in his eye and the hard line of his mouth.

When Adam spoke his exasperation was thinly veiled.

"Barney," he sighed, "When it comes to ops I'm not much of a believer in giving people the benefit of the doubt. I regard any result short of dropping a complete bomb load on the nail as a defeat. It takes years to train a crew to fly a Lanc. It costs tens of thousands of pounds to build that Lanc. It is all for nothing if a crew doesn't do the job over the target, and I won't have that. I will not have my crews bombing open country when they've been detailed to bomb a town. Nor, for that matter, will I have my crews jettisoning any part of their bomb load to gain height on the way to the target. A crew which fails to complete an operation, which fails to press on, betrays all the other chaps who do press on. I agree, it's bloody bad luck if a crew's camera is on the blink but believe me, from now on every crew will make damned sure their camera is in a-one working order before the off!" Adam took a breath, instantly resumed the attack. "When a crew fails to bomb the target we've risked seven lives and a valuable aircraft for nothing.

Absolutely nothing. I will not have that!" He walked on, picking up his pace. "That's why I won't take anybody's word that they've bombed the target unless they can prove it. We're not playing cricket, Barney. If you get caught out in this game there's no second innings. No second chance. You're either dead or stuck in a Stalag Luft for the duration."

That evening the Mess had organised a dance.

Adam, keen to avoid being labelled a prig on his first day at the station, made a token appearance. He departed after half-an-hour but not before being drawn onto the dance floor by a winsome, red-haired Section Officer. 'Do you dance, sir?' The WAAF had asked, speculatively, as the new Wingco sipped gingerly at his pint of warm, frothy beer. The next thing he knew the woman was in his arms. Or rather, clinging to him at arm's length on the dance floor. Fortunately, the red-haired WAAF was as terrified of him as he was of her, and she had disengaged herself at the first opportunity, disappearing into the anonymous throng immediately the band paused for breath. He had finished his beer and beaten a hasty tactical retreat to his office.

In the morning he planned to crawl over his new home with a fine toothcomb, stick his nose into every nook and cranny of his new command, and to talk to as many of his people, both aircrew and erks as he could find. Tonight, he skimmed methodically through a hundred files, poring uneasily over the still warm coals of Bert Fulshawe's unhappy and ultimately doomed reign at Ansham Wolds.

Bert had lost his sense of humour and probably, his grip on reality in the weeks before his death. Bert's policy had been to carpet all early returners, come down hard on any pilot reporting a problem with his aircraft. Without exception. Failure to complete an op for any reason was invariably deemed to have occurred 'due to a lack of determination to press on'. The day before his death Group had screened him and formally asked him to account for the poor performance of 647 Squadron, citing the squadron's unusually high rate of early returns and below average aircraft serviceability figures. In their way, such requests were fairly routine. Some Squadron Commanders took them to heart, most with a pinch of salt. However, in Bert's case, coming the day he had been screened, it may have been the straw that finally broke the proverbial camel's back. Insult heaped upon injury, beyond human forbearance.

Adam smoked, gazed at Helen Fulshawe's cigarette case. He thought of Helen naked, breathless, giggling in his arms. He shook his head, remembered her dressed in sober navy blue at her baby daughter, Kate's christening with Bert proudly at her side. With an effort he composed his thoughts, steeled himself, and began to write.

Dear Helen,

I used to think Bert was indestructible. I never thought that one day I would end up attempting to fill his shoes.

I wish there was something I could say or do to bring Bert back. I know it sounds terribly cruel but when these things happen the only thing one can do is say one's goodbyes and try to carry on. Bert would want you to get on with your life. You have Jack and Kate, and your memories.

I'm sorry. I'm not much use. Too accustomed to locking my feelings away, not allowing myself to let the hurt show, I suppose. I wish I could cry sometimes, the trouble is if I let myself cry for all the fine fellows I've known who've gone for a burton, I might never stop.

All I can do now is tell you what happened.

647 Squadron has had a bit of a sticky spell lately. Nobody's fault, just bad luck. Bert, being Bert, was doing all he could to hold things together. You know, leading from the front, showing the chaps what's what, making sure everybody pressed on regardless.

On Wednesday Bert briefed his crews to attack Hanover. A big show, maximum effort - all available kites. As his Lancs were taking off one crew reported a problem. Bert being Bert went to find out what the problem was. When he got to the aircraft he decided the problem wasn't that serious and that he would fly the op. Typical Bert!

So, to cut a long story short, Bert took off and flew the op. Unfortunately, something went wrong, we don't know what. Bert was forced to come back early before he had a chance to jettison his bombs. To make matters worse when he got back over the airfield one of his engines was on fire and by then it was too low for his crew to bale out. Engine fires are rotten things. Even when the extinguisher works, the fire often restarts. You always lose the engine, and even if the wing isn't badly damaged the control surfaces tend to get jammed. Basically, unless you've got lots and lots of altitude to play with and plenty of time for the chaps to bale out, engine fires are very dicey things.

Bert tried his best but there was a crash. Bert and his crew were killed instantly; they probably wouldn't have known what happened. They certainly wouldn't have felt any pain.

Bert died leading from the front. He died trying to do the right thing. The honourable thing. I know that's how he'd like to be remembered and it is the way I shall always remember him. He said to me once: 'Wouldn't it have been awful if we'd bought it on that Wilhelmshaven show? Think what we'd have missed and what great fun we wouldn't have had!'

If I may, I must mention one or two practical matters. The Committee of Adjustment Officer will be forwarding Bert's personal effects to you in due course. If there is any delay or anything is missing, please let me know so that I can expedite things.

I gather that in Bert's Will he asked that in the event of his death in England, he should like to be buried locally in Lincolnshire. I believe he thought this would lessen your pain. Group Captain Alexander informs me that the local

Rector and Bert were firm friends, and that the funeral was conducted with full honours and solemnity by the Reverend Simon Naismith-Parry.

When, in due course, you feel ready to visit Bert's grave you must let me know so that I can make all the necessary arrangements. I know travelling can be difficult, and so can finding somewhere to stay, but let me know if and when you want to come up to Lincolnshire and leave it to me to sort things out. You must let me know if there is anything I can do to help you in these sad days.

I'm so sorry Bert's gone. I shall miss him terribly. Try to be strong for the children.

All my love,
Adam.

Chapter 12

Sunday 26th September, 1943
RAF Ansham Wolds, Lincolnshire

Flight-Lieutenant Peter Tilliard was waiting for Adam when he returned to his office after Morning Song in the station chapel. The pilot stood rigidly at attention before his Squadron Commander's desk. He was ashen-faced, unsteady on his feet.

Adam viewed him thoughtfully.

Tilliard was the fifth man to request a personal interview.

The previous four had packed their bags and departed Ansham Wolds within an hour of speaking to him, each man spirited off the station lest he contaminate his fellows. Aircrew knew the rules, understood exactly what awaited them if they asked to be transferred to ground duties: demotion, humiliation, shame.

Bomber Command called it LMF, or more correctly the 'lack (of) moral fibre'. Nobody talked about it, for it was hardly a suitable topic for polite conversation. The RAF did not recognise combat fatigue - let alone outright fright - as an honourable exemption from flying ops. The squadrons quarantined LMF defaulters like plague carriers, got rid of them at the earliest moment. Few LMF cases ever came before a full court-martial, in fact formal proceedings were wholly exceptional events. When a man reneged on his 'contract' with Bomber Command the drill was to inflict the summary injustice of loss of rank and honour without a word uttered in his defence. Once branded with the LMF iron a man was cast adrift, shuffled from depot to depot, his waking hours filled with menial, demeaning, futile tasks, shunned and despised.

It was a scandal and no doubt, one day Bomber Command would be called to account. In the meantime, for his part Adam tried to give every man a fair hearing. It was the least that *any* man who had flown ops deserved.

'I'm sorry, sir,' one trembling boy, a sprog gunner in a B Flight crew, had apologised. 'I can't go on. The last op, over Hanover, I saw a fighter and I froze. It went for another Lanc a couple of hundred yards away and I just watched. I couldn't do anything. The chaps had to drag me out of the turret when we got back. They covered up for me but I know if that fighter had gone for us they'd all be dead now and it would be my fault.'

Adam had no reason disbelieve the boy. 'Do you realise what you're letting yourself in for?' He asked. It was a question he always asked.

'I think so, sir.'

Adam stopped short of condemning him out of hand. Instead, he marked his file 'application for transfer to ground duties approved with immediate effect'. The boy was ordered to report to the Group depot for assessment and posting. If the Wing-Commander (P) was so inclined, the boy might be given a second chance.

'I don't like the odds, sir,' admitted the next interviewee, an experienced navigator from Barney Knight's Flight. 'I don't want to go on flying.' The navigator's pilot had followed him into the office. Both men had weighed the odds and decided that Russian roulette was not for them. Adam had noted their papers 'transferred to ground duties with immediate effect (LMF)'.

While he could find it in his heart to sympathise with a man who was genuinely terrified out of his wits every time he flew an op, he had no time for a man who had simply lost their appetite for the fight. Such men were beneath contempt.

'It's my wife, sir,' began the fourth defaulter, Barney Knight's mid-upper gunner. He was close to tears. 'She's just had a baby. I can't stop thinking about what would happen to her if anything happened to me. The skipper's the best. I ain't never flown with anybody who can do the things he can do. I don't know what to do, sir. I can't stop thinking about what happened to Mickey.'

'Who was Mickey?' Adam inquired, tersely.

'He was our tail-end charlie, sir. We'd come through together, all the way from basic training to OTU to here, sir. Twenty-two ops, sir. Coming back from that last Berlin show we got jumped by a fighter and Mickey bought it. We never found the top half of him. They had to hose what was left of him out of the turret. I can't close my eyes without seeing the blood. I'm not a coward, sir. I'm not. I'm not!'

'Have you spoken to Squadron Leader Knight about this?'

'Oh, no, sir. I couldn't. It wouldn't be right, would it?'

Adam had signed a chit assigning him 'to ground duties, pending assessment of his future suitability for flying duties'. He had attached a personal note to the Wing-Commander (P) reminding him of the gunner's 'exemplary operational record' and requesting that he be 'notified immediately of the outcome of the assessment process'. If the Wing-Commander (P) wanted a quiet life and the gunner was very, very lucky, he might find himself posted to an Operational Training Unit as an instructor. More likely, he would lose his stripes, find himself square-bashing.

Perhaps, that was the kindest thing. If he was sent to an OTU, sooner or later he would be asked to fly ops, again. In Bomber Command when a man was granted a second chance, there was always a price to be paid.

Courage, Adam reflected, was a fleeting commodity. On the squadrons a casual acceptance that whatever will be, will indeed be was a priceless asset. Fatalism was the semi-official religion of Bomber Command aircrew. On ops a vivid imagination was a corrosive thing, an awful millstone. Some men were stronger than others. Lucky men learned to put the nightmares to one side; the damned became the prisoners of their fear.

'Squadron Leader Knight wouldn't understand, sir.'

Adam did not argue the point.

The new Wingco was a stranger to the gunner, and it was easier to admit defeat to a stranger than it was to a friend. The man was racked with guilt because by requesting a posting to ground duties he was breaking not only his own unwritten contract with Bomber Command, he was letting his pilot down and betraying his comrades.

Privately, Adam had expected as many as a dozen men to request a transfer to ground duties.

When a Squadron had a really bad trot a

tour of thirty operations became a death sentence. According to that morning's flight roster he had eighteen complete crews and thirty or so other variously qualified, unassigned flying personnel under his command, about one hundred and sixty aircrew. That only four men had chosen life over death was humbling. Rain drummed against the windows; and beat out an insistent, staccato rhythm on the corrugated iron roof.

"Well, spit it out!" Adam ordered Flight-Lieutenant Peter Tilliard.

He was disappointed to see him. Disappointed but not wholly surprised. Four nights ago Bert Fulshawe had killed his crew and understandably, the poor fellow had probably concluded that his situation at Ansham Wolds was intolerable. Adam blamed himself. He ought to have taken Tilliard aside earlier and tried to put his mind at rest.

"I'd like to request a transfer to another Squadron, sir."

Out of courtesy Adam contemplated the request. But only for a moment. Then he rejected the idea out of hand.

"Request denied!"

"Sir?"

"Dammit, there's no need to stand there like a toy soldier. For goodness sake sit down before I get a crick in my neck!"

Tilliard removed his cap, sat stiffly in the nearest chair. "I'm sorry, sir," he blurted out. "I don't understand. I rather assumed you'd want to see the back of me as soon as possible."

Adam groaned. "Oh, I see. So that's what this nonsense is about!" He drew out his cigarette case, offered it to the other man.

"I don't, thank you, sir."

"It is Peter, isn't it?"

"Yes, sir."

"You look dreadful, by the way." Adam knew Tilliard had been in the base hospital, grounded with an ear infection for the last week. The man was still on the sick list and was likely to remain on it for some days.

"A little feverish, sir. I'll be right as rain in a day or two."

"Weren't you with Freddie Tomlinson at Marston Grange last year?"

"Yes, sir. I didn't think you'd remember me."

Adam half-smiled.

"Freddie said you were one of his best pilots. Freddie's a pretty good judge of these things." Tilliard blushed, shifted uncomfortably under his CO's gaze. Adam lit his cigarette, sat back. Tilliard had every right to be down in the dumps. But not for ever.

"Anyway," he went on. "If you think I'm about to let a chap of your calibre swan off to another squadron you've got another thing coming!"

"Oh, I see."

His CO frowned at him, dismissed him.

"You must put this behind you, Peter. Get on with the job in hand. Now get out of here and stop wasting my time!"

Chapter 13

Sunday 26th September, 1943
RAF Ansham Wolds, Lincolnshire

Peter Tilliard opened his eyes slowly, and very cautiously because his skull felt as if there was somebody inside it swinging a hammer against his temples. He squinted, waiting for the world to come into sharper focus. Very, very slowly, he began to make sense of his surroundings. He was in a white-washed room, and the stench of disinfectant was pervasive, over-powering.

"Ah, not dead after all, then," remarked a familiar voice.

"Where am I, Mac?" Tilliard croaked, turning towards the sound of Flight Lieutenant Ewan McDonald's voice. His Flight Commander was grinning ruefully, cradling a mug in his hands. The smell of cocoa vied unsuccessfully with that of disinfectant.

"The hospital. You are an idiot, you know!"

"Hospital? What happened?"

"You ran out in front of the Groupie's car. You're damned lucky to be in one piece! Scared the Groupie's driver half to death. Poor girl. Took me an age to convince her you weren't dead. She was in a terrible state!"

"Oh." Tilliard thought about it. "I went to

see the new Wingco, I think? Didn't I?"

"Yes."

"He told me to stop wasting his time and to get on with the job in hand? Or words to that effect?"

McDonald sipped his cocoa. "Aye. That's what he told me."

"A car? I don't remember that?"

"Well, you'll have to take my word for it!"

Tilliard became aware that certain parts of his anatomy were paining him more than others. He ached all over but his ribs were overly sore and his right ankle throbbed unmercifully. He groaned.

McDonald shook his head, ruefully.

"The flight surgeon says you've got a couple of cracked ribs and you might have broken your ankle. He hasn't developed the x-ray yet. Otherwise you're more or less okay. It's a good thing you've got such an incredibly thick skull or you'd have more than just a headache, now."

When the accident happened McDonald had been on his way to present A Flight's training program to Wing-Commander Chantrey. Arriving on the scene Tilliard had looked awful and the Group Captain's WAAF driver was inconsolable. His friend could easily have been killed. Instead, he had got away with little more than a few cuts and bruises. Perhaps, it was an omen. A sign that the ill luck dogging Ansham Wolds these past months was changing for the better. He desperately wanted to believe it.

McDonald had stopped off at the infirmary after having spent the last hour discussing the new training programme with the Wingco. Chantrey had been pragmatic, businesslike, utterly on top of the essentials. He had added a series of minor suggestions, points to be included in the schedules, and scrawled 'approved' on McDonald's plans. They had exchanged brief pleasantries about the trials and tribulations of being a Flight Commander, whereupon the Wingco had dismissed him and strolled off into the distance with Rufus.

"So, I got knocked down by a car?"

"Yes, you idiot!"

Despite his discomfort this struck a comic chord in Tilliard's befuddled brain. He grimaced, would have laughed but for the stabbing pains across his chest. The irony of the situation was sublime. Of all the many and varied ways a fellow could get himself killed in Bomber Command, getting run down in broad daylight by the Station Master's car was one of the ways he could claim, with absolute honesty, to have never previously contemplated.

"Ah, back in the world of the living,"

commented the Flight Surgeon, entering armed with a clipboard. He seemed a little irritated. "As if we don't have enough really sick people to look after! I thought you pilot chappie's were supposed to look where you're going? What on earth were you thinking? Giving that poor girl a shock like that?"

"What poor girl?"

"The Groupie's driver!" McDonald reminded him.

"Pretty little thing," the Flight Surgeon said. "Damned pretty, actually. You'll be glad to hear that your ankle isn't broken. Just bruised, badly sprained, that's all. However, you've got a couple of cracked ribs. And concussion. Fairly mild, I'd say. You must have a pretty thick skull. You'll probably be back in the air in a fortnight." He reconsidered. "Well, say three weeks, to be on the safe side."

"Three weeks," Tilliard groaned, unhappily.

"Right," McDonald declared. "I'm off. Try and have a nap, Peter. Take it easy while you can, eh." The room went quiet. Tilliard closed his eyes. He tried to doze, without much success. Sometime later there was a timid knock at the door.

"Hello," whispered a woman's voice.

Tilliard opened his eyes.

Her face drifted in and out of focus. She

seemed familiar but no name crossed his befuddled mind. She tip-toed into the room, glancing over her shoulder.

"Hello," he muttered, forcing his swollen lips into what he hoped was a grinning shape.

"I'm," the girl began, hesitantly. She was petite, blond, pale, biting her lower lip, and standing at the foot of the bed. "I'm the one who knocked you over."

"Oh, I see."

"I had to come and see how you were, I was so worried."

"I'm alright, really," he declared, hoarsely. "Why are we whispering?"

"I'm not supposed to be here."

"Oh, right."

"They said I couldn't visit you, you see," she explained. "Because you're an officer, and I'm not, I think."

"Oh." Her face swam into sharp focus and Tilliard found himself staring into her cornflower blue eyes. "But you came, anyway?"

She shrugged, half-smiled and glanced uneasily over her shoulder.

"That was awfully brave of you," he decided.

Again, she shrugged and said nothing.

"It was all my fault," he assured her. "The Wingco had just given me a pep talk and I was full of beans. I can't have been looking where I was going."

"I'm just glad you're not too badly hurt. You're not, badly hurt, I mean?"

The man shook his head which was a mistake because it prompted a sudden dizziness. For a moment he thought he was going to be sick but the nausea passed. He saw the woman's concern, raised a hand.

"No, I'm okay. Really, I am."

"I better go."

"Yes. It wouldn't do to get into any trouble on my account."

She edged towards the door.

"I'll go, then."

"You mustn't get caught." He realised he was gazing into her soft blue eyes, mesmerized.

"Don't worry, I won't."

"Thank you for coming to see me."

She slipped away.

"Damn," Tilliard sighed. "You clot! You didn't ask her name! Oh, you absolute clot!"

Chapter 14

Monday 27th September, 1943
Thurlby-le-Wold Station, Lincolnshire

Adam lit a cigarette and strolled onto the bleak northern platform. He was late and so was the train. He cast a jaundiced eye at the sky, convinced that the weather was taunting him. Overhead the clouds were dark and sombre, threatening rain and a stiff breeze gusted fitfully down the length of the wholly exposed platform. The cold knifed through his greatcoat.

Last night the Main Force had mounted a maximum effort attack on Hanover. 38 heavies were missing and according to Pat Farlane's ops people, the early indications were that the main bombing concentration had probably been several miles north of the city centre.

Ansham Wolds had sat out the raid, the AOC having rescinded his undertaking to allow 647 Squadron to continue to operate, at half, or flight-strength. Adam had protested vigorously. Whereupon Pat Farlane had picked up the scrambler phone.

'Look,' Pat explained. 'The AOC has spoken. I'm afraid that's that!' Adam had demanded to speak to the Group Commander.

Unavailingly, Pat had tried to talk him out of it. 'On your head be it, old man,' he had cautioned, eventually promising to pass his 'request' up the chain of command. Shortly afterwards, Adam had been summoned back to the scrambler phone to 'explain' himself to the AOC's deputy.

Air Commodore Crowe-Martin had not been amused. In fact he had been hopping mad, marshalling words like 'impertinence', 'arrogance' and 'insubordination' - this last word no fewer than four times - in the course of a brief, heated, yet marvellous spirited and succinct dressing down. It seemed the AOC was of the opinion the Officer Commanding No. 647 Squadron was making a 'damned nuisance of himself', and that he was 'to desist forthwith'. Adam had bitten his tongue, thanked the Deputy Group Commander for his advice and undertaken to bear it in mind in future.

'Make sure you do!' He was told.

This morning the Lancaster Force had been alerted for a 'Goodwood', another maximum effort operation. Once again, Ansham Wolds had been excluded from the order of battle. This time Group Captain Alexander had grabbed his elbow, taken him aside: 'Look, it doesn't do to get too worked up about these things, my boy. Don't be a chump. Rome wasn't built in a day, you know. I'm sure the chaps at Group know what they are doing. Our time will come. Mark my words, our time will come.' The Old Man was adamant. There would be no repeat of yesterday's 'tantrums'. Under protest but respectfully, Adam had deferred to his Station Master's wishes.

He was still brooding unhappily on the iniquities of the world when he was caught unawares by a woman's voice.

"Excuse me!" The voice splintered his darkling thoughts. A woman's gentle, well-meaning voice. "Excuse me. I hope you don't think I'm being forward, but aren't you Wing-Commander Chantrey?"

He turned around.

"Adam Chantrey?" The voice belonged to a dark, slim woman of about thirty. Two children, a boy of about six or seven and a girl of three or four clung to her arms. Adam could not place her face. This troubled him because had ever met her before he would surely have recollected it now. She was winsome, strikingly attractive. Her smile was like a breath of spring air.

"Er, yes. That's me," he confessed, shedding a little of his preoccupation. Her eyes were brown. Hazel brown and full of a warmth that cut through his habitual reserve like a hot knife through butter.

"I thought so the moment you walked onto the platform." She smiled and Adam went to pieces. His defences came crashing down, he was at her mercy. "Oh, I'm sorry. I'm Eleanor. Eleanor Grafton. I'm the schoolmistress at Ansham Wolds."

"Oh, I see." Of course, he saw nothing. He was blind to practically everything except her smile and bewitched by her brown eyes. "I'm new at Ansham Wolds. I haven't got around to visiting the village, yet."

She laughed, realising he had no idea who she was.

"You were my brother's commanding officer at Kelmington."

"Your brother?"

"David Merry."

"You're Dave's sister?" Flight-Lieutenant Dave Merry had been shot down a year ago - almost to the day - flying one of Adam's Lancasters to Wismar; an old-fashioned sort of raid by less than a hundred 5 Group Lancasters. One aiming point was situated in the middle of the town, another in the nearby Dornier factory. Some of his crews had bombed from as low as two thousand feet that night. Dave's aircraft had been attacked by a fighter on the way home. With shrapnel wounds to his legs he had crash-landed his aircraft in a field. Adam pictured his friend's face, recollected snatches of conversations long forgotten. "You're Dave Merry's sister?" He checked, stupidly.

Again, she laughed.

"His big sister. I recognized you from a photograph of you and David. I think it was taken at Boscombe Down. Sometime last year."

"My word. It's a small world isn't it?"

"Isn't it," Eleanor agreed. "He talked about you a lot in his letters. It probably sounds silly but even though we've never met, I feel I already know you quite well. Dave said we'd get on famously if we ever met. Oh, forgive me," she said, quickly. "What must you think of me?"

"No, it's alright. Really."

"It's just such a surprise meeting like this."

"Absolutely," he mumbled. He gestured at the youngsters. "Your children?"

She smiled and proudly introduced the boy and girl.

"This little horror is Jonathan, and this is Emily. Say 'hello' to Wing-Commander Chantrey, children." This they did, shyly, reluctantly.

Adam forgot himself and patted the boy's fair head. Such was his disorientation that he was completely unaware that he was not alone in his sudden enchantment.

Eleanor looked away, flushing with embarrassment. What was she thinking? Gabbling on so? What must he think of her? 'Dave said we'd get on famously?' Whatever was she thinking of telling him that? She tried to take stock, to catch her breath. It had never occurred to her that the real Adam Chantrey could be so young and yet so careworn, old before his time. Or have such gentle eyes. She forgot herself. Horrified by her temerity, she heard herself speaking with the voice of another woman, a stranger.

"If you don't mind me saying so, Wing-Commander; you really don't look very well?"

As soon as she said it she cursed her ineptitude, her rudeness. It was unforgivable. She was hugely relieved when the man seemed to find nothing whatsoever untoward in her remark.

"I think I'm coming down with a cold. Must stop flying around with the window open," he joked. "I'll survive. I always do. It's what I do best."

"Oh."

"Sorry," he said, instantly, fearing he had given offence. "Polite conversation is not my forte. Out of practice, you see. Not that much call for it in my line of work."

Eleanor shone her smile on him and he basked in its warmth.

"You must be meeting somebody, too?"

"Yes. I've just taken over 647 Squadron. I'm meeting my Navigation Leader."

"Would that be Ben? Ben Hardiman?"

"Yes, I insisted Ben and the rest of my crew took some of the leave they were due... And you?" Dave Merry and Ben had been illustrious drinking partners.

"I'm meeting my father. He's a sort of scientist, I suppose," Eleanor explained, not suspecting for a moment that Adam and her father were old sparring partners. "He lives in London but every now and then I bully him into spending a few days in the country. You know, to get away from things. We've been waiting for ages. His train's late."

Adam retrieved a cigarette from his silver case. He was in no mood to encounter Professor Charles St John Merry. The scar tissue from his last skirmish with the Prof was still too fresh and the imminent prospect of crossing swords with the old curmudgeon took the edge of his sudden good cheer. They heard the faraway sound of a train approaching.

"Your husband's away?" He glanced down the tracks, cursing his insensitivity. It was obviously the wrong thing to ask and he should have known it from the start.

"Harry was killed in the desert," Eleanor said, without fuss. "At El Alamein."

"Sorry. Things can't be easy for you." He left it at that. Death was a thing he was used to, something that called for no comment.

Eleanor pursed her lips. It was as if he intuitively understood that she neither wanted nor needed anybody's pity. She was reeling, now. Dreaming. Any minute she would wake up but waking up was the last thing she wanted to do. "The trains are always late, these days," she remarked, battling to retain her composure.

Adam scratched his chin.

"It wouldn't happen in Germany. Sometimes I wonder if that's what all this is really about. You know, our inalienable national right to run our trains without reference to a timetable."

When Eleanor laughed the man took his courage in his hands, met her eye, and dared to smile a smile of his own. For her part the woman noted how the smile took years off him, brought his grey-blue eyes to life.

"I think you're trying to make fun of me, Wing-Commander."

"Do you mind?"

The train was puffing, clanking, creaking into the station. Eleanor was breathless. The boyish directness of his question had grabbed her whole attention. She shook her head.

"No. I don't mind at all."

Adam did not trust himself to speak.

The train juddered to a squealing halt and its three over-crowded carriages began to disgorge passengers. Ben Hardiman, leaning out of the window, spotted the couple from afar. His friend and a strikingly attractive, raven-haired woman, standing still amidst the throng; successive waves of humanity swept past the man and the woman who only had eyes for each other. Ben tossed his bags to the ground and jumped down. Straightening to his full height, a good head above the next tallest man on the platform, he stretched his cramped limbs and gathered up his kit. Much to his amusement Adam Chantrey was so preoccupied with his lady-friend that he failed to notice his approach. The big man eyed the woman and her children as the crowd thinned around them.

"Why, it must be Ellie? Dave Merry's sister?"

"And you must be Ben," Eleanor laughed. "I recognised the Wing-Commander from Dave's photograph album. What a co-incidence? Meeting like this after all this time?"

A few minutes later the two men bade Eleanor and her children farewell, and left them waiting for the Sheffield train. They were silent until they got to the Bentley.

"I hope I wasn't interrupting anything," Ben chortled as Adam gunned the motor.

His friend threw him a blank look.

"Back there? The fetching schoolmistress?"

"Don't be dim!"

"Sorry I spoke."

Adam sent the car skidding onto the road.

"No Rufus?" Ben prompted, presently.

"Adjutant's keeping an eye on him. The Adjutant's a chap called Tom Villiers, he seems a good sort, by the way."

"Oh, right." Ben Hardiman absorbed the information. Every posting had new pitfalls to ensnare the unwary. It was always good to have one's card marked in advance, and to know exactly whom one might rely on from the outset. "We on for ops tonight?"

"No. Fancy stopping off for a pint on the way back?"

The Boar's Head in Broughton, a sedate, fifteen minute drive from Ansham Wolds, was virtually empty when the two men walked in. Adam ordered beers and they retreated to a corner, settling on rough hewn benches.

"Happy landings?" Ben proposed.

"I'll drink to that."

"You look bloody awful, by the way," he commented, matter of factly.

"So I've been told. Head cold, that's all."

They supped their ale.

"How did Maureen take the news when you told her you were coming up here?" Adam prompted.

"Philosophically, as always," came the flat reply. Ben rarely spoke of his family, the wife and the young daughters to whom he was devoted. He kept ops and the normal world in separate compartments. Every old lag tended to develop their own way of coming to terms with things. To each their own. Ben had chosen one way, Adam another. "So what's Ansham Wolds like?"

"Cold, wet and miles from anywhere." Adam reported, deadpan.

"What about the natives? Friendly?"

"Some friendlier than others."

"That's to be expected." Ben drained his jug. "Anybody we know from elsewhere?"

Adam shook his head.

"No. The Station Master's a brick. One of the Flight Commanders, Mac, he's got an old head on his shoulders. Oh, and there's a chap called Peter Tilliard. On his second tour. He was a Lindholme instructor."

"The name rings a bell," Ben Hardiman grunted. "Are you ready for another pint, skipper?"

Adam nodded, watched his friend depart for the bar.

"Bombs away!" He decided, returning with

two fresh pints.

They drank. "What about the other Flight Commander? Barney Knight? I hear he's supposed to be a rising star?"

Adam pursed his lips, thought about the question.

"Ask me again in a month's time," he suggested, thoughtfully. "From what I can gather Barney was Bert's right hand man. Given what happened to Bert and the Squadron, that didn't work so well. We shall see."

Ben accepted the logic of this. Sentimentality was not going to be allowed to blur Adam Chantrey's decisions. He had been sent to Ansham Wolds to pick up the pieces and there was no room on a failing Squadron for prima donnas. Nor was there scope to assuage bruised pride.

"You think we'll have problems with Barney Knight's old lags?"

Adam shook his head. "No. Nothing like that. But things will be easier when they understand Barney doesn't have all the answers."

His friend raised his glass to his lips, drank long.

"No objections to me fraternising with the enemy?"

"No," a brief chuckle, flickering amusement

in his grey eyes. "Feel free to put out peace feelers."

"Fair enough," the big man acknowledged. He changed the subject. "So Dave Merry's sister lives in Ansham?"

"So it would seem."

Ben winked at his friend. "Judging by the way you were looking at each other, you two hit it off straight away?"

Adam's cheeks coloured.

The other man, witnessing his unease, was intrigued. It confirmed his original diagnosis. The lovely Eleanor had discovered a chink in the low-level king's armour, irrefutable proof that he was as human as the next man. Adam Chantrey was smitten. Not head over heels; he was not that sort of chap. But smitten he was and there was no denying it. Smitten moreover, by the daughter of his *bête noire*, the perfidious Prof. The irony of the situation was sublime. The chaps in the crew would not believe a word of it but they had never known the skipper in the old days, and therefore had no inkling that the Wingco was anything but the celibate, monkish figure that he so assiduously presented to the world.

"I suppose her husband's off doing his bit for King and Country in some distant and disease-ridden outpost of Empire?" Ben pressed, determined to extract every last ounce of flesh from the situation.

Adam knew he was being ribbed. Normally, he would have endured it with a rueful smile. Not so today.

"He's dead," he growled, slamming the door in his friend's face. "The poor chap bought it in North Africa."

[The End]

Author's End Note

Thank you for reading **Main Force Country**. I hope you enjoyed it; if not, I am sorry. Either way, I still thank you for giving of your time and attention to read it. Civilisation depends on people like you.

Although all the events depicted in the narrative of **Main Force Country** are set in a specific place and time the characters in it are the constructs of my own imagination. *Ansham Wolds, Waltham Grange, Kelmington* and *Faldwell* are fictional Bomber Command bases, likewise, *380, 388* and *647 Squadrons* exist only in my head. While *Bawtry Hall* was the Headquarters of No 1 Group, I have made no attempt to accurately depict it, or any members of the command staff posted to it in 1943 and 1944. Moreover, the words and actions attributed to specific officers at Bawtry Hall and elsewhere are *my* words.

One final thought.

A note on jargon. I have been at pains to make **Main Force Country** accessible to readers who are relatively new to the subject matter and therefore not necessarily wholly conversant with the technologies and contemporary Royal Air Force 'service speak'; while attempting *not* to sacrifice the atmosphere and *reality* of that subject matter for readers who are already immersed in Bomber Command's campaigns. For example, I describe aircraft by employing their designated 'letters' – that is, B-Baker, or T-Tommy and so on – rather than using the common RAF parlance of referring to an aircraft by its serial number. Likewise, where possible I look to explain technical terms and procedures in layperson's language. Inevitably, this leaves one open to the charge that one is 'dumbing down'; but there are many trade-offs in writing any serious work of fiction, and I sincerely hope I have drawn the line in more or less the right place. However, this is a judgement I leave to you, my reader.

Other Books by James Philip

The Timeline 10/27/62 World

The Timeline 10/27/62 - Main Series

Book 1: Operation Anadyr
Book 2: Love is Strange
Book 3: The Pillars of Hercules
Book 4: Red Dawn
Book 5: The Burning Time
Book 6: Tales of Brave Ulysses
Book 7: A Line in the Sand
Book 8: The Mountains of the Moon
Book 9: All Along the Watchtower
Book 10: Crow on the Cradle
Book 11: 1966 & All That

A standalone Timeline 10/27/62 Novel

Football In The Ruins – The World Cup of 1966

Coming in 2018-19

Book 12: Only In America
Book 13: Warsaw Concerto

Timeline 10/27/62 - USA

Book 1: Aftermath
Book 2: California Dreaming
Book 3: The Great Society
Book 4: Ask Not of Your Country
Book 5: The American Dream

Timeline 10/27/62 – Australia

Book 1: Cricket on the Beach
Book 2: Operation Manna

Other Series & Books

The Guy Winter Mysteries

Prologue: Winter's Pearl
Book 1: Winter's War
Book 2: Winter's Revenge
Book 3: Winter's Exile
Book 4: Winter's Return
Book 5: Winter's Spy
Book 6: Winter's Nemesis

The Harry Waters Series

Book 1: Islands of No Return
Book 2: Heroes
Book 3: Brothers in Arms

The Frankie Ransom Series

Book 1: A Ransom for Two Roses
Book 2: The Plains of Waterloo
Book 3: The Nantucket Sleighride

The Strangers Bureau Series

Book 1: Interlopers
Book 2: Pictures of Lily

NON-FICTION CRICKET BOOKS

FS Jackson
Lord Hawke

**Audio Books of the following Titles
are available (or are in production) now**

Aftermath
After Midnight
A Ransom for Two Roses
Brothers in Arms
California Dreaming
Heroes
Islands of No Return
Love is Strange
Main Force Country
Operation Anadyr
The Big City
The Cloud Walkers
The Nantucket Sleighride
The Painter
The Pillars of Hercules
The Road to Berlin
The Plains of Waterloo
Until the Night
When Winter Comes
Winter's Exile
Winter's Nemesis
Winter's Pearl
Winter's Return
Winter's Revenge
Winter's Spy
Winter's War

Cricket Books edited by James Philip

The James D. Coldham Series
[Edited by James Philip]

Books

Northamptonshire Cricket: A History [1741-1958]
Lord Harris

Anthologies

Volume 1: Notes & Articles
Volume 2: Monographs No. 1 to 8

Monographs

No. 1 - William Brockwell
No. 2 - German Cricket
No. 3 - Devon Cricket
No. 4 - R.S. Holmes
No. 5 - Collectors & Collecting
No. 6 - Early Cricket Reporters
No. 7 – Northamptonshire
No. 8 - Cricket & Authors

Details of all James Philip's books and forthcoming publications
will be found on his website www.jamesphilip.co.uk

Cover artwork concepts by James Philip
Graphic Design by Beastleigh Web Design

Printed in Poland
by Amazon Fulfillment
Poland Sp. z o.o., Wrocław